Louis XV

MONSIEUR

DE CHAUVELIN'S WILL

BY

ALEXANDRE DUMAS.

Fredonia Books
Amsterdam, The Netherlands

Monsieur de Chauvelin's Will

by
Alexandre Dumas

ISBN: 1-4101-0047-2

Reprinted from the 1898 edition

Fredonia Books
Amsterdam, The Netherlands
http://www.fredoniabooks.com

INTRODUCTORY NOTE.

MONSIEUR DE CHAUVELIN'S WILL.

In "Monsieur de Chauvelin's Will" we are introduced to several of the historical characters who play parts of some prominence in the first of the so-called Marie-Antoinette Romances, the "Memoirs of a Physician," and to one — the Duc de Richelieu — who had been a leading figure at court and in society from the very beginning of the century, and whom the author has introduced, as a young man, in the "Regent's Daughter," and, a few years later, in "Olympe de Clèves," lending a willing hand in the work of corrupting the young Louis XV., and launching him upon the path which he followed so consistently to the last ghastly hour of his deplorable life.

The historical element is not more prominent in any of the author's historical romances than in the one before us. As the characters, almost without exception, are historical personages, so it may be said that there is authority for almost every incident of the narrative. Indeed, those chapters which deal with the life at court at the close of

the long reign of Louis XV., the ill-feeling between the low-born favorite and the ill-fated
Marie-Antoinette, the constantly recurring inci-
dents which were looked upon by the king as
ominous of his impending death, the indecorous
dissensions at his bedside between the factions of
the Duc d'Aiguillon and the Duc de Choiseul, the
unclerical conduct of the Archbishop of Paris, and
the details of the closing scenes, illumined by the
heroic devotion of the despised and neglected princesses and the blind priest, — those chapters read
like so many pages from some of the many historical works of the school to which the reign of
Louis XV. seems to offer peculiar attractions.
Imbert de Saint-Amand, Arsène Houssaye, and the
De Goncourts occupy prominent positions among
the writers of that school, and most of the inci-
dents here described were deemed deserving of a
place in their pages.

The Abbé de Beauvais, Bishop of Senez, was the
Lenten preacher at court in 1773 and 1774, and
much surprise was felt that the bold and outspoken
language of his sermons did not prevent his appointment to the bishopric. The threatening pas-
sage from the sermon preached on Holy Thursday
— "Forty days more, sire, and Nineveh will be
destroyed!" — is historical. Houssaye says that
Louis died on the fortieth day,[1] and the De Goncourts cite a work entitled "Interviews in the
Other World," wherein Louis XV. is represented

[1] Arsène Houssaye: "Galerie du XVIIIe Siècle. — Louis XV."

as saying to the Prince de Conti: "You are well aware, cousin, that it was that infernal sermon on Holy Thursday, 1774, that killed me."[1]

"The mirror surmounted by two Cupids holding a crown" is mentioned by the authors last quoted as forming a part of a whole toilet set in solid gold for which the order was given to Roettiers (Rotiers), but which was never completed.

The same authors refer to the project of the favorite to persuade the pope to annul her marriage with the Comte du Barry. "He" (the Abbé du Terray) "gave substance to the chimera held up moment- arily before the imagination of the favorite by the chancellor and the Duc d'Aiguillon: the annulment of her marriage with the Comte du Barry and a marriage of conscience with the king."

The Marquis de Chauvelin actually existed, but his name is connected only with the pleasures of the king. Like Richelieu and D'Ayen, he has no place in serious history. "One evening" — we quote the brothers De Goncourt once more — "when Louis XV. was playing at piquet with Madame du Barry, and the Marquis de Chauvelin, his old friend and former companion in dissipation, was leaning upon the back of his chair, Madame du Barry raised her eyes and said: 'Why, Monsieur de Chauvelin, what a face you are making!' The king turned: Chauvelin fell dead at his feet."

Many different stories were circulated to explain the attack of smallpox, all having some connec-

---

[1] E. & J. de Goncourt: "La du Barry."

tion with the king's persistence in the evil courses
in which he had indulged so long, but Voltaire tells
us that there was an epidemic of the disease in the
neighborhood and that the king fell a victim to it.

There is no lack of authority for the scandalous
scenes about the bedside of the dying monarch, as
described by Dumas, or for the grewsome details
of the closing hours of his life. Shocking as all the
circumstances of his death were, one cannot avoid
a feeling that it was a fitting end for the selfish,
heartless, weak, pleasure-loving king, who had
taken for his motto: "After me the deluge!" and
whose life seemed to be governed by no other
sentiment than that therein implied. The deluge
came after him, largely through his instrumentality,
and it was fitting that he should have a foretaste
of the suffering in store for the innocent victims of
his misgovernment and oppression.

LIST OF CHARACTERS.

Period, 1774.

———◆———

LOUIS XV., King of France.

THE DAUPHIN, afterwards LOUIS XVI.

MARIE ANTOINETTE, the Dauphiness.

DUC DE RICHELIEU,
MARQUIS DE CHAUVELIN,
DUC D'AIGUILLON,
DUC DE CHOISEUL, } of the French Court.
DUC D'AUMONT,
DUC DE LA VRILLIÈRE,
DUC DE COIGNY,
DUC D'AYEN,

COMTESSE DU BARRY, the King's mistress.

CHON, her sister.

CHRISTOPHE DE BEAUMONT, Archbishop of Paris.

MONSIEUR DE LORRY, Bishop of Tarbes.

CARDINAL DE LA ROCHE-AYMON.

THE BISHOP OF CARCASSONNE.

ABBÉ DE LAVILLE.

ABBÉ DE BROGLIO.

MONSIEUR DE SARTINES.

MONSIEUR LAMARTINIÈRE, the King's first surgeon.

MONSIEUR BONNARD, } physicians to the King.
MONSIEUR BORDEU,

MARQUISE DE CHAUVELIN, wife of Marquis de Chauvelin

LIST OF CHARACTERS.

Père Delar, her spiritual director.
The Children of Monsieur and Madame de Chauvelin
Abbé de Villenave, their tutor.
Bonbonne, steward of Marquis de Chauvelin.
A Courier of the King.
La Gourdan.
Sophie Arnould, an actress.

ILLUSTRATIONS.

———

CONTENTS.

———◆———

MONSIEUR DE CHAUVELIN'S WILL.

MONSIEUR DE CHAUVELIN'S WILL.

———◆———

I.

As you go from Rue du Cherche-Midi to Rue Notre-Dame des Champs, you may notice at your left, facing a fountain at the corner of Rue du Regard and Rue de Vaugirard, a small house entered on the municipal registers as Number 84.

And now, before going farther, let me make a confession which I hesitated to make. Although I was welcomed in that house with the most open-hearted friendship, almost from the day of my arrival from the provinces; although for three years it was like my brother's house to me; although in all my griefs or joys, I might safely have knocked at the door of that house with my eyes closed, certain that it would open to my tears or my smiles; nevertheless, I was compelled, in order to state its location accurately to my readers, to locate it myself on a map of the city of Paris.

Mon Dieu! who would have believed it twenty years ago?

The fact is that, during the last twenty years, such a multiplicity of events, like a constantly rising tide, has

1

extinguished in the men of our generation the memories
of their youth, that they no longer remember with the
memory,— the memory has its twilight in which far-off
souvenirs fade away,— but with the heart.

And so, when I lay aside my memory and take refuge
in my heart, I find there, as in a consecrated tabernacle,
all the treasured souvenirs which have escaped one by one
from my life, as the water trickles drop by drop through
the cracks in a vase; in the heart there is no twilight
growing ever darker and darker, but a constantly brighten-
ing dawn.   The memory tends to darkness, that is to say
to nothingness; the heart tends to light, that is to say to
God.

However, the little house is there, surrounded by a
gray wall behind which it is half hidden, — for sale, so I
am told, on the point of escaping from the hospitable
hands that opened its doors to me, alas!

Let me tell you how I first came to enter those doors.
That will lead us — by a roundabout path, I know — to
the story I have to tell you; but no matter, come with
me, we will talk as we follow the path, and I will try to
make it seem shorter to you than it really is.

It was toward the close of 1826, I think.   I spoke
of an interval of twenty years only, and it is twenty-
two years since, you see.   I was then twenty-three years
old.

I have told you of my literary dreams, apropos of poor
James Rousseau.   Even as early as 1826 they had become more ambitious.   I was no longer writing " La Chasse
et l'Amour " in collaboration with Adolphe de Leuven ; nor
was I then at work upon " La Noce et l' Enterrement " with
Vulplan and Lasaagne : I was dreaming of " Christine "
all by myself.   A lovely dream ! a glowing, resplendent
dream, which, in my juvenile hopes, was to open to me

the garden of the Hesperides, the garden with the golden fruit of which Criticism is the attendant dragon.

Meanwhile, poor Hercules that I was, Necessity had placed a world on my shoulders. An evil-minded goddess is that same Necessity, for she had not even, as in poor Atlas' case, the excuse of desiring to rest for an hour by crushing me.

No, Necessity crushed me — me and many others — as I crush an anthill. Why? Who knows? Because I happened to be under her feet and because the cold goddess with the iron nails, having a bandage over her eyes, did not see me.

The world that she had placed upon my shoulders was my office desk.

I earned a hundred and twenty-five francs a month, and for that hundred and twenty-five francs this is what I was obliged to do.

I went to my office at ten o'clock; I left at five; but I returned in the evening at seven and remained till ten.

Why that extra amount of labor, in the summer, at that hour in the evening, that is to say, at the very time when it would have been so pleasant to breathe the pure air of the country or the intoxicating atmosphere of the theatres?

I will tell you why: The Duc d'Orléans' portfolio had to be made up.

That aide-de-camp of Dumouriez at Jemappes and Valmy, that outlaw of 1792, that professor at the college of Reichenau, that explorer of Cape Horn, that citizen of America, that prince who was the friend of the Foys, the Manuels, the Laffittes, and the Lafayettes, that king of 1830, that exile of 1848, was in 1826 still called the Duc d'Orléans.

It was the happy period of his life; as I had my

dream, so he had his. My dream was success for my work; his dream was the throne.

O my God! have compassion on the king! O my God! grant peace to the gray-haired man! O my God! give to the husband and father all the paternal and conjugal happiness that are still possible, in the infinite treasures of thy loving-kindness!

Alas! at Dreux, I saw bitter tears flow from the eyes of that crowned father on the tomb of the son who was to wear a crown.

Is it not true, sire, that the loss of your crown did not cost you so many tears as the death of your child?

Let us return to the Duc d'Orléans and his portfolio.

That portfolio contained the day's mail and the evening papers, which had to be sent to Neuilly.

And then, when the portfolio had been despatched by a courier on horseback, we had to await the reply.

The latest comer in the office was assigned to that task, and, as I was the latest comer, it was divided between myself and one other. My colleague Ernest Banet was detailed to make up the morning portfolio. We alternated in making up the portfolio on Sunday.

So it was that on a certain evening, after despatching the portfolio and while awaiting the messenger's return, I was scratching off a few lines of "Christine," when the office door opened, a shapely head, covered with light, curly hair, appeared in the opening, and a voice with a slightly mocking accent emitted, in tones that approached shrillness, the three monosyllables, —

"Are you there?"

"Yes," I answered quickly. "Come in."

I had recognized Cordelier Delanoue, who was, like myself, the son of a former general of the Republic, and, also like myself, a poet. Why has he been less successful than I in the career we have followed together? I have no idea. He certainly has a brighter intellect than mine, and he writes undeniably better poetry.

Everything in this world is a caprice of chance, good luck or bad luck. Not till we are dead shall we know which of us two, he or I, has had the good luck or the bad luck.

Cordelier Delanoue's visit was a bit of good fortune. Like all the people I have loved, I loved him then and I love him today; but I love him more than I did, and I am sure that it is the same with him.

He came to ask me if I cared to go to the Athénée to hear a dissertation upon some subject or other.

The dissertator was Monsieur de Villenave.

I knew Monsieur de Villenave by name only. I knew that he had made a translation of Ovid that was highly esteemed, and that he had formerly been secretary to Monsieur de Malesherbes and tutor of Monsieur le Marquis de Chauvelin's children.

At that time, the play or diversion of any sort was a very infrequent experience with me. All the doors of theatres and salons which have since been thrown open to the author of "Henri III." and "Christine" were closed to the clerk on a salary of fifteen hundred francs, whose duty it was to make up Monsieur le Duc d'Orléans' evening portfolio. I accepted, and requested Delanoue to await the courier's return with me.

While we were waiting he read me an ode he had written. It was a preparation for the séance at the Athénée.

The courier returned; I was free, and we bent our steps toward Rue de Valois.

It would be impossible for me to tell you in what part of Rue de Valois the meetings of the Athénée were held;

that was the only time, I believe, that I ever went there. I never cared much for such functions, where a single person does the talking and everybody else listens. The subject must needs be very interesting or very unfamiliar, the person who speaks on that subject must needs be very eloquent or very picturesque, for me to find any attraction in that uncontroverted discourse, when contradiction would be contrary to propriety and criticism discourteous.

I have never been able to listen uninterruptedly to an orator or preacher. There is always some corner of the discourse upon which I catch, and which causes my thought to make a halt while the discourse goes on. Having once halted, I naturally begin to look at the subject from my own point of view; so that I make my speech or my sermon in an undertone while he is making his aloud. When we have both reached the end, we are often a hundred leagues apart, although we started from the same point.

It is the same with plays. Unless it be the first performance of a play written for Arnol, Grassot, or Ravel, that is to say, of a work which is completely out of my own line and which I frankly confess my inability to produce, I am the worst "first-nighter" imaginable. If the play is an imaginative one, the characters no sooner appear than they cease to be the author's creations and become my own. In the first *entr'acte* I take them, I appropriate them. Instead of waiting for what is to come in the remaining four acts, I introduce them into four acts of my own composition; I make the most of their characters, I utilize what there is original about them. If the *entr'acte* lasts no more than ten minutes, that is more than I need to build for them the card-house into which I induct them, and it is the same with my dramatic card-house as with the discourse or the sermon of which I spoke just now. My card-house is almost never identical with the author's, so that, as I have made a reality of my dream, it is reality that seems a dream to me, a dream which I am all ready to combat, saying, "Why, that's not right, Monsieur Arthur.— Why, that's not right, Mademoiselle Honorine. — You go too fast or too slow; you turn to the right instead of to the left; you say yes when you ought to say no. Oh! oh! oh! why, this is unendurable!"

With historical plays it is much worse. I naturally have in my head my own play all thought out upon the subject treated; and as it naturally is constructed with all my faults, that is to say with abundance of details, with absolute rigidity of characters, and with a double, triple, or quadruple plot, it very rarely happens that my play bears the remotest resemblance to the one that is being played. Wherefore something that furnishes entertainment to others becomes simply torture to me.

Now my confrères are warned; if they invite me to the first performance of their plays now, they know on what conditions I attend.

I did that evening for Monsieur de Villenave what I do for everybody else; however, as I arrived when his lecture was three-fourths done, I began by looking at him instead of listening to him.

He was at that time a tall old man, sixty-four or sixty-five years old, with hair of the purest silver, a pale complexion, and bright black eyes. There was in his dress that sort of absent-minded neatness characteristic of the man who dresses once or twice a week, no more, and during the balance of the time sits about in the dust of his study, in an old pair of trousers, an old dressing-gown, and a pair of old shoes. It is the duty of the wife or the daughter, of the housekeeper in fact, to make ready the

holiday costume, with the frilled shirt and ruffle, and the
starched white cravat.   Hence the species of protest
entered by that well-beaten, well-brushed costume against
the every-day costume, which, for its part, has a horror
of the bamboo switch and the whisk-broom.

Monsieur de Villenave wore a blue coat with brass
buttons, black trousers, a white waistcoat, and a white
cravat.

A strange mechanism that of the thought, — intellectual
machinery which goes or stops regardless of what we may
do, because it is God's hand that sets it up; a clock,
which strikes, at the bidding of its caprice, the hours of
the past and sometimes those of the future.

Upon what did my mind stop as I looked at Monsieur de Villenave? Was it, as I said just now, upon
a corner of his discourse? No, but upon a corner of
his life.

I had read at some time — where, I have no idea — a
pamphlet by Monsieur de Villenave, published in 1794,
entitléd : " Relation de Voyage de 132 Nantais."

It was on that episode of Monsieur de Villenave's life
that my mind caught, so to speak, when I saw Monsieur
de Villenave for the first time.

Monsieur de Villenave had, as a matter of fact, lived at
Nantes in 1793, at the same time that Jean-Baptiste
Carrier of bloody memory lived there.

There he had seen the proconsul, deeming the trials too
long and the guillotine too slow, suppress the trials,—which
were entirely useless, by the way, as they never saved the
accused, — and substitute for the guillotine the boats with
airholes.   He may perhaps have been on the quay on the
Loire on the 15th November, 1793, when Carrier, as an
initial test of his *republican baths* and *vertical banishment*
— such were the names he bestowed upon the new style

of punishment invented by him — caused ninety-four priests to embark, on the pretext that they were to be taken to Belle Isle. He may have been on the bank of the river when the horrified current cast upon the bank the dead bodies of the ninety-four men of God. He may then have revolted at that spectacle, which, being renewed every night, after a little time so corrupted the water of the river that the people were forbidden to drink it. Perhaps he was even more imprudent than that, and went so far as to give Christian burial to some of those first victims, who were destined to be followed by so many others. At all events it came to pass that Monsieur de Villenave was arrested one morning and cast into prison, and was destined, with his companions, to do his part toward corrupting the river, when Carrier changed his mind. He selected a hundred and thirty-two prisoners and despatched them to Paris, as a mark of homage from the provincial scaffolds to the guillotine at the capital; but doubtless that mark of homage failed to satisfy him, for he sent orders to Captain Boussard, commanding the escort, to shoot his hundred and thirty-two prisoners on arriving at Ancenis.

Boussard was a good fellow, so he did nothing of the sort, but kept on towards Paris.

Carrier, being apprised of his failure to obey, despatched orders to Hentz, a member of the Convention, who was proconsul at Angers, to arrest Boussard when he arrived there, and to throw the hundred and thirty-two Nantes men into the water.

Hentz had Boussard arrested; but when it came to drowning the hundred and thirty-two prisoners, the brass of his revolutionary heart, which seems not to have been of triple thickness, melted, and he ordered the victims to march on toward Paris, — a proceeding which caused

Carrier to remark, shaking his head contemptuously, '*A poor drowner*, that Hentz, *a poor drowner !*"

And so the prisoners continued their journey. Out of a hundred and thirty-two, thirty-six died before reaching Paris, and the ninety-six who did arrive, arrived, luckily for them, just in time to testify at the trial of Carrier, instead of answering as defendants upon their own trial.

The 9th Thermidor had come, the day of reprisals had dawned, the turn of the judges to be judged had arrived, and the Convention, after a month's hesitation, had ordered the prosecution of the *great drowner*.

The result was that, at the memory of the pamphlet which Monsieur de Villenave had published thirty-two years before, in his prison, I allowed my thoughts to wander back over the past, and what I saw, what I heard, was no longer a literary address, delivered by a professor at the Athénée, but a terrible, scathing, deadly arraignment of the strong by the weak, of the judge by the accused, of the executioner by the victim.

And so great is the power of the imagination that hall, spectators, tribune, all were transformed : the lecture-room of the Athénée became the hall of the Convention ; the peaceful auditors were changed to wrathful avengers, and the eloquent professor with the smooth-flowing periods was thundering forth a public accusation, demanding the death penalty, and bewailing the fact that Carrier had but a single life, wretchedly inadequate to pay for the fifteen thousand lives he had cut short.

And I seemed to see Carrier, with his lowering stare, shattering the accusation with his glance, and to hear him crying in his strident voice to his former colleagues, —

"Why blame me to-day for what you ordered me to do yesterday ? Why, in accusing me the Convention accuses itself. My condemnation will be the condemnation of you all ; remember that ! You will all be included in the proscription that includes me. If I am guilty, then everything in this room is guilty ; yes, everything, everything, everything, even to the president's bell."

But, in spite of all that, they voted upon his fate ; in spite of it all, he was condemned. The same terror which had guided the action guided the reaction, and the guillotine, after drinking the blood of the condemned, impassively drank the blood of the judges and executioners!

I had let my head fall between my hands, as if it were repugnant to me, execrable homicide though the man was, to see him suffer the death he had inflicted so freely upon humanity.

Delanoue touched me on the shoulder.

" It is done," he said.

" Ah ! " I replied, " is he executed ? "

" Who ? "

" That abominable Carrier."

" Yes, yes, yes," said Delanoue, "and it 's a good thirty-two years since that little misfortune happened to him."

" Ah ! you did well to wake me," I said. " I was having a nightmare."

" So you were asleep, eh ? "

" At all events I was dreaming."

" The devil !   I won't tell Monsieur de Villenave that. I am going to take you to his house to have a cup of tea."

" Oh ! you can tell him if you choose ; I will describe my dream, and he won't be offended."

Thereupon Delanoue, still uncertain whether I was really awake or not, led me from the empty lecture-room into a reception-room, where Monsieur de Villenave was receiving the congratulations of his friends.

There, I was presented in the first place to Monsieur de Villenave, then to Madame Mélanie Waldor, his daughter, then to Monsieur Théodore de Villenave, his son.

After that we all repaired on foot, by the Pont des Arts, to Faubourg Saint Germain.

After half an hour's walk we reached our destination and disappeared, one after another, in that house on Rue de Vaugirard which I mentioned at the beginning of this chapter, and of whose interior I propose to give a description, after a short sketch of its external aspect.

II.

A PASTEL BY LATOUR.

THE house had an individuality of its own, borrowed from that of the man who lived in it.

We have said that the walls were gray; we should have said that they were black.

You entered the premises through a large gate, cut in the wall, directly adjoining the porter's lodge; you then found yourself in a garden without flower-beds, trodden everywhere, with trellises without grapes, arbors without shade, trees almost without leaves. If a flower did happen to grow in a corner, it was one of those wild flowers, which are almost ashamed to show themselves in the city, and which, mistaking that dark, damp enclosure for a little desert, had grown up there by mistake, believing itself farther than it really was from the habitations of men, only to be plucked at once by a lovely, rosy-cheeked child, with fair curly hair, who seemed a cherub fallen from heaven and out of place in that out-of-the-way corner of earth.

From the garden, which was some forty or fifty feet square, and which ended in a broad, paved strip adjoining the house, you entered a tiled corridor.

Upon that corridor, at the end of which was a staircase, four doors opened : on the left, the doors of the dining-room and kitchen ; on the right, the door of a small room, and the door leading to the pantry and offices.

This ground floor, which was dark and damp, was hardly occupied except at the hours for meals.

The real dwelling, that to which we were taken, was the first floor.

On the first floor were the landing, a small salon, a large salon, Madame Waldor's bedroom and Madame de Villenave's bedroom.

The salon was noticeable both in shape and furnishing.

It was oblong in shape with a console and a bust in each corner.

One of the busts was of Monsieur de Villenave.

Between the two busts at the farther end, on a console facing the fireplace, was the most important work of art and archæology in the salon.

It was the bronze urn which had contained Bayard's heart; a small bas-relief on its circumference represented the chevalier *sans peur et sans reproche* lowering the hilt of his sword.

Next came two large pictures : one by Holbein, a portrait of Anne Boleyn ; the other by Claude Lorraine, representing an Italian landscape.

I believe that the two frames which hung opposite those pictures contained, one a portrait of Madame de Montespan, and the other a portrait of Madame de Sévigné or Madame de Grignan.

Of furniture upholstered in Utrecht velvet there were for the friends of the family capacious couches with thin white arms, and for strangers easy-chairs and ordinary chairs.

This floor was Madame Waldor's special domain, and there she exercised her vice-royalty.

We say her vice-royalty, because although her father had abandoned that salon to her, she was in reality only vice-queen there. As soon as Monsieur de Villenave entered he resumed his sovereignty, and thenceforth the reins of the conversation were in his hands.

There was something despotic in Monsieur de Ville-nave's character, displayed in his intercourse with strangers as well as with his family. You felt, on entering his house, that you belonged to the man who had seen so much, studied so much, who, in a word, knew so much. That despotism, tempered as it was by the courtesy of the master of the house, nevertheless, weighed oppressively upon the company as a whole. Perhaps the conversation was *more skilfully guided*, as they used to say, when Monsieur de Villenave was present, but it certainly was less free, less amusing, less clever, than when he was not there.

It was just the opposite with Nodier's salon. The more Nodier was at home the more at home every one else felt.

Luckily Monsieur de Villenave rarely came down to the salon. He passed most of his time in his own quarters, on the second floor, and on ordinary days did not appear until dinner; and after dinner, when he had talked for a moment, when he had moralized a little with his son, and scolded his wife a little, he stretched himself out in his arm-chair, closed his eyes while his daughter put his hair in curl-papers, and then went up to his own apartments again.

That quarter of an hour during which the teeth of the comb scratched his head gently, was the daily quarter of an hour of beatitude in which Monsieur de Villenave allowed himself to indulge.

But why those curl-papers? the reader will ask.

In the first place, perhaps they were only an excuse for having his head scratched. In the second place, Monsieur de Villenave was, as we have said, a fine old man who must once have been a fine young man, and his face with its strongly marked features was superbly framed in those waves of white hair which brought boldly in relief the brilliancy of his great black eyes.

In fact, we must admit that Monsieur de Villenave, although a student, was inclined to be coquettish, but coquettish with his head, nothing more.

In other respects his appearance mattered little to him. Whether his coat was blue or black, whether his trousers were full or tight, whether the toe of his boot was round or square, all such questions concerned his tailor and his boot-maker, or rather his daughter, who attended to all those details.

If his hair was well dressed that was enough for him.

When his daughter had put on his curl-papers — an operation which was performed invariably between eight and nine o'clock at night — Monsieur de Villenave took his candlestick and went upstairs.

It is Monsieur de Villenave in his own sanctum, *at home* as the English say, whom we propose to try to describe, with little hope of success.

The second floor was divided into vastly more compartments than the first; it consisted of a landing adorned with plaster busts, an anteroom, and four other rooms.

We will not characterize those rooms as salon, bedroom, dressing-room, and study. Little Monsieur de Villenave cared for all those superfluities! No : there were five rooms for books and boxes, — that is the whole story.

Those five rooms contained some forty thousand volumes and four thousand boxes.

The anteroom in itself formed an immense library. It had two exits : the one on the right led into Monsieur de Villenave's bedroom, which bedroom itself opened, through a corridor by the alcove, into a large closet lighted by inside windows ; the one on the right opened into a large room, which, in turn, opened into a smaller one.

This large room which opened into the smaller one not
only had, as did its neighbor, its four walls covered with
bookcases filled with books and supported by foundations
of boxes, but a very ingenious structure had been set up
in the middle of each of the two rooms, similar to the
affair sometimes placed in the centre of a salon so that
people can sit all around it. Thanks to that structure
the centre of the room, forming a library within a
library, left free only a quadrangular space in which not
more than one person could circulate freely. A second
person would have impeded the circulation ; and so it
rarely happened that Monsieur de Villenave admitted
anybody, even an intimate friend, to that *sanctum
sanctorum.*

A few privileged ones may have put their heads in at
the doors, and, through the learned dust that floated constantly in luminous atoms in the infrequent sunbeams
which found their way into that tabernacle, have descried
the bibliographic mysteries of Monsieur de Villenave, as
Claudius, by virtue of his feminine disguise, was en-
abled to surprise some of the mysteries of the kindly
goddess Isis from the atrium of her temple.

That was where the autographs were : the epoch of
Louis XIV. alone filled five hundred volumes.

There too were the papers of Louis XVI., the correspondence of Malesherbes, four hundred autographs of
Voltaire, two hundred of Rousseau. There were the
genealogies of all the noble families of France, with their
alliances and their proofs of nobility. There were the
drawings of Raphael, Jules Romain, Leonardo da Vinci,
Andrea del Sarto, Lebrun, Lesueur, David, and Lethière ;
the collections of minerals too, rare books on plants, and
unique manuscripts.

There, in short, was the labor of fifty years, engrossed

2

day after day by a single thought, absorbed hour after hour by a single passion, — the passion, at once so ardent and so gentle, of the collector, wherein the collector puts forth all his intelligence, and upon which his pleasure, his happiness, his very life depend.

Those two rooms were the precious ones. Certainly Monsieur de Villenave, who, many times, had almost given his life for nothing, would not have parted with the contents of those two rooms for a hundred thousand crowns.

There remained the bedroom and the dark room, situated at the right of the anteroom and extending back parallel to the two we have described.

The first of the two was Monsieur de Villenave's bedroom, in which the bed was certainly the least important article, being buried in a recess closed by two doors in the wainscoting.

That was the room in which Monsieur de Villenave received.

If it were absolutely necessary, you could walk there; likewise if it were absolutely necessary, you could sit down.

This is the way in which it was possible to sit down, and these the circumstances under which it became possible to walk.

The old servant — I have forgotten her name — would partly open Monsieur de Villenave's door and announce a visitor.

The opening of the door always surprised Monsieur de Villenave in the midst of a classification, a fit of musing, or a nap.

" Well ! what is it, Françoise ? " — Let us suppose that her name was Françoise. — " Great heaven ! can't I be left in peace for an instant ? "

" *Dame !* monsieur," Françoise would reply, " I had to come."

" Well, tell me quickly : what do you want of me ? How is it that you always come just at the moment when I am the busiest ? — Well ! "

And Monsieur de Villenave would raise his great eyes heavenward with a despairing expression, fold his hands and heave a sigh of resignation.

Françoise was used to the stage-setting ; she would allow Monsieur de Villenave to go through with his pantomime and his *asides*. And when he had finished,—

" Monsieur," she would say, " Monsieur *So-and-so* has come to make you a little call."

" I am not at home ; go."

Françoise would open the door slowly ; she knew what was coming.

" Wait, Françoise," Monsieur de Villenave would call to her.

" Yes, monsieur."

And she would open the door again.

" You say that it 's Monsieur *So-and-so*, Françoise ? "

" Yes, monsieur."

" Oh, well ! let him come in, and, if he stays too long, you can come and tell me that some one wants me. Go, Françoise."

Françoise would close the door.

" Oh! *mon Dieu ! mon Dieu !* would any one believe it ? " Monsieur de Villenave would murmur. " I never disturb anybody, and yet somebody must needs disturb me constantly."

Françoise would open the door once more to admit the visitor.

" Ah! good morning, my friend," Monsieur de Villenave would say. " Glad to see you; come in,

come in. It's a long while since we've seen you.
Pray sit down."

"On what?" the visitor would ask.

"Why, on whatever you choose, *pardieu!* On the
couch."

"I would gladly do so, but "— Monsieur de Villenave would glance at the couch.

"Ah! yes, true. It's covered with books," he would
say. "Oh, well! Move up an easy-chair."

"It would give me great pleasure, but — "

Monsieur de Villenave would pass his easy-chairs in
review.

"True," he would say. "But what can I do, my
dear fellow? I don't know where to put my books.
Take a common chair."

"I would ask nothing better, but — "

"But what? Are you in a hurry?"

"No, but I don't see that there are any more common
chairs vacant than arm-chairs."

"It's incredible," Monsieur de Villenave would say,
throwing up his arms. "It's incredible! Wait!"

He would leave his seat, groaning inwardly, care-
fully lift from a chair the books that rendered it useless, deposit the books on the floor where they added
another molehill to the twenty or thirty similar ones
scattered over the floor, and move the chair beside his
own easy-chair, that is to say, to the corner of the
hearth.

I have told you under what circumstances one could
sit down in that room. I will proceed to tell under
what circumstances you could walk about there.

It sometimes happened that just as the visitor entered,
and after the indispensable preamble we have repeated,
— it sometimes happened, we say, that, by a double

combination of chances, the door into the alcove and the door of the corridor leading to the closet behind the alcove were both open. At such times the visitor could see in the alcove a pastel representing a young and pretty woman holding a letter in her hand, the picture being lighted by the light from the window in the corridor.

Thereupon, if the visitor had any conception of art, — and it rarely happened that they who called on Monsieur de Villenave were not artists in some direction, — he would exclaim, —

" Oh, monsieur ! what a beautiful pastel ! "

And he would start to go from the hearth to the alcove.

" Wait ! " Monsieur de Villenave would exclaim, " wait ! "

Indeed, you could see that two or three molehills of books, toppling against each other, formed a sort of counterscarp of curious shape, which it was necessary to cross before reaching the alcove.

Thereupon Monsieur de Villenave would rise and lead the way, and, as a skilful miner opens a trench, he would open through the lines of typography a tunnel which made it possible to reach a point in front of the pastel, which itself faced the bed.

Having reached that point, the visitor would repeat, —

" Oh ! what a beautiful pastel ! "

" Yes," Monsieur de Villenave would reply, with the air of the ancient court which I have never noticed in any one but him and two or three old men of fashion like him, " yes, it 's a pastel by Latour. It represents an old friend of mine, who is no longer young ; for, as well as I can remember, when I knew her in 1784.

she was five or six years older than I. We have never met since 1802, but that does not prevent our writing to each other every week and receiving our weekly letters with equal pleasure. Yes, you are right, it is a charming pastel, but the original was much more charming. Ah!"

And a ray of youth, as soft as a reflection of the sun, would pass over the handsome old man's beaming face, making him look forty years younger.

And very often, in the last-mentioned case, Françoise would have no need to make the false announcement that her master was wanted, for, if the visitor had any sense of delicacy, he would very soon leave Monsieur de Villenave absorbed in the reverie to which the sight of that lovely pastel of Latour had given birth.

III.

THE LETTER.

Now how had Monsieur de Villenave collected that fine library?

How had he made that collection of autographs without parallel in the world of collectors?

With the labor of his whole life. In the first place Monsieur de Villenave had never burned or destroyed a letter or a paper.

Notices of meetings of the learned societies, invitations to weddings, notices of funerals, — he had kept them all, classified them all, and each had its place. He possessed a collection of every imaginable thing, even of the volumes which had been snatched half-burned from the flames in the courtyard of the Bastille on the 14th of July.

Two men were constantly employed hunting for autographs for Monsieur de Villenave. One was a man named Fontaine, whom I knew, and who was himself the author of a book entitled "Le Manuel des Autographes." The other was a clerk in the Ministry of War. All the grocers in Paris were familiar with those two indefatigable visitors, and put aside for them all the papers they bought. They would make a selection from the papers, and buy them at fifteen sous the pound, Monsieur de Villenave paying them thirty sous.

Sometimes too Monsieur de Villenave would make an expedition on his own account. There was not a grocer in Paris who did not know him, and who, when he saw him coming, did not get together the material for bags and horns of plenty to submit it to his learned investigation.

It goes without saying that, on the days when he went out for autographs, Monsieur de Villenave went out also for books. The indefatigable bibliophile would follow the line of the quays, and there, both his hands in his trousers' pockets, his tall body bent forward, his fine face lighted up by the longing for a lucky find, he would gaze eagerly into the depths of the show-windows, in quest of the unknown treasure. He would turn the leaves over for an instant, and when the book proved to be the one he had sighed for, when the edition was the one he was in search of, the book would leave the dealer's stall, — not to take its place in Monsieur de Villenave's library. In Monsieur de Villenave's library there was no room, and had been none for a long while, and it was necessary to make room by exchanging books for drawings or autographs. No, the book would take its place in the garret, which was divided into three compartments: one for octavos at the left, one for quartos at the right, one for folios in the centre.

There was the chaos out of which Monsieur de Villenave proposed some day to make a new world, something like an Australia or a New Zealand.

Meanwhile they lay on the ground, piled one upon another, in semi-darkness.

That garret was the limbo where the souls were confined whom God sends neither to heaven nor to hell, because he has designs upon them.

One day, without any apparent cause, the poor house trembled to its foundations, groaned, and cracked. The terrified occupants thought that there had been an earthquake and rushed into the garden.

Everything was peaceful, in earth and sky. The fountain continued to play at the corner of the street. A bird was singing in the highest branches of the tallest tree.

The disaster was only partial. It proceeded from some secret, mysterious, unknown cause.

They sent for the architect.

The architect examined the house, sounded the walls, asked many questions, and ended by declaring that the accident could have had no other cause than an overstrain.

Accordingly he asked leave to inspect the garret.

But that request was met with vigorous opposition on the part of Monsieur de Villenave.

What was the explanation of that opposition, which yielded at last in face of the architect's firmness?

It was that Monsieur de Villenave felt that his hidden treasure, the more precious to him in that he was almost unacquainted with it, was exposed to great risk by that visit.

Indeed, in the middle chamber alone they found twelve hundred folios weighing almost eight thousand pounds.

Alas! he had no choice but to sell those twelve hundred folios, which had made the house sag, and which threatened to pull it down.

That painful operation took place in 1822. And in 1826, when I first knew Monsieur de Villenave, he had not recovered from that blow, and more than one sigh, of which his family knew neither the cause nor the purpose, went in pursuit of those dear folios, collected by him with such infinite pains, and now, like children driven from the paternal roof, wandering about, orphaned, and dispersed over the face of the earth.

I have said how kind and sweet and hospitable the house on Rue de Vaugirard was to me: on the part of Madame de Villenave, because she was naturally affectionate; on the part of Madame de Waldor, because, being a poet, she was fond of poets; on the part of Théodore de Villenave, because we were of the same age, and both at the age when one feels the need of giving away a portion of his heart and of receiving a portion of the hearts of others.

Lastly, on the part of Monsieur de Villenave, because, although I was not a collector of autographs, I possessed, thanks to my father's military portfolio, an interesting collection of them. For, as my father held high rank in the army from 1791 to 1800, having thrice been general-in-chief, he had been in correspondence with all those who had played prominent parts during those years.

The most interesting autographs in that correspondence were those of General *Buonaparte.* Napoléon did not long retain that Italianized name. Three months after the 13th Vendémiaire he adopted the French form, and signed himself *Bonaparte.* My father had received during that brief period five or six letters from the young general of the interior. That was the title he assumed after the 13th Vendémiaire.

I gave Monsieur de Villenave one of those autographs flanked by one of Saint-Georges, and one of the Maréchal de Richelieu; and, by virtue of that sacrifice, which was a pleasure to me, I was admitted to the privileges of the second floor.

Little by little I became sufficiently intimate in the house for Françoise to cease announcing me to Monsieur de Villenave. I used to go up alone to the second floor. I would knock at his bedroom door, open at the words, " Come in! " and was almost always well received.

I say almost always, because great passions have their hours of tempest. Suppose a collector of autographs, who has long coveted a precious signature, — a signature of Robespierre, for instance, who left only three or four; of Molière, who left only one or two; of Shakespeare, who, I believe, left none at all; and suppose that, just as he has his hand on that unique or almost unique signature, it eludes our collector's grasp by some accident or other. Naturally he is in despair.

Enter his room at such a moment, though you be his father, his brother, or an angel, and you will see how you will be received; unless, by the way, being an angel, you exert your divine power to produce the signature that had no existence, or to duplicate the signature of which there is but one known example.

Such were the exceptional circumstances under which I was ungraciously received by Monsieur de Villenave. Under any other circumstances I was sure of finding a pleasant face, a ready mind, an obliging memory, even during the week.

I say "during the week," because Sunday was set aside for scientific visitors at Monsieur de Villenave's.

All the foreign bibliophiles and cosmopolitan collectors of autographs who came to Paris never failed to pay a visit to Monsieur de Villenave, as vassals go to do homage to their sovereign.

Sunday was the day for exchanges. By means of those exchanges, Monsieur de Villenave completed his foreign collections, for which his grocers were insufficient, abandoning to the German, English, or American collectors some parings of his magnificent French material.

So I was admitted to the house. I was received first on the first floor, and in due time on the second. I had obtained the right of entry there every Sunday; and lastly, I had been granted the privilege of going there whenever I chose, a privilege which I shared with two or three others at most.

Now, on a certain week day, a Tuesday I think, I called upon Monsieur de Villenave to ask leave to study an autograph of Christine, — for I like, as you know, to form an opinion of the character of my personages from the style of their handwriting; one day, I say, I called upon that errand, about five o'clock in the afternoon, and rang at the door. I asked for Monsieur de Villenave, and was admitted.

As I was passing through the door, Françoise called me.

"What is it, Françoise?" I asked.

"Is monsieur going to call on the ladies or on monsieur?"

"I am going up to monsieur's room, Françoise."

"Very well, if monsieur was very good he would spare my poor legs two flights of stairs and give Monsieur de Villenave this letter, which has just arrived for him."

"Willingly, Françoise."

Françoise gave me the letter, and I went upstairs.

When I reached the door I knocked as usual, but there was no reply.

I knocked a little louder.

Still no reply.

I knocked a third time, and that time with some uneasiness, for the key was in the door, and the presence

of the key in the door invariably indicated the presence
of Monsieur de Villenave in his room.

I ventured, therefore, to open the door, and I saw
Monsieur de Villenave drowsing in his easy-chair.

At the noise I made, or perhaps because of the current of air that entered with me and disturbed certain
magnetic currents, Monsieur de Villenave gave a sort
of cry.

"Oh! I beg your pardon," I said. "I beg your pardon
a thousand times. I was careless; I disturbed you."

"Who are you? What do you want?"

"I am Alexandre Dumas."

"Ah!"

And Monsieur de Villenave breathed again.

"Really, I am in despair," I added, "and I will go."

"No," said Monsieur de Villenave, heaving a sigh,
and passing his hand across his forehead, "no, come in."

I went in.

"Take a seat."

By some chance a chair was vacant. I took it.

"How strange it is!" he said. "As you saw, I was
dozing. The twilight has come. Meanwhile, my
fire has gone out. You waked me. I found myself in
an unlighted room, and could not explain the sound
that had disturbed my sleep. Doubtless it was the air
from the door blowing on my face. But it seemed to
me that I saw a great white cloth floating in the air,
something like a shroud. How strange it is, is it
not?" continued Monsieur de Villenave, with the
shuddering movement of the whole body which indi-
cates that one is cold. "But it was you, I am happy
to say."

"You say that to set my mind at rest concerning my
awkwardness."

"No, really not. I am very glad to see you. What have you there?"

"Ah! I beg your pardon, I forgot. A letter for you."

"So! an autograph? Whose is it?"

"No, it's not an autograph; it's simply a letter, at least so I imagine."

"Oh! yes, a letter!"

"A letter that came by post and was given me by Françoise to bring to you. Here it is."

"Thanks. Just put out your hand, please, and give me — "

"What?"

"A match. Really, I am still as dull and confused as possible. If I were superstitious, I should believe something was going to happen."

He took the match I handed him and lighted it in the hot ashes on the hearth.

As it burned, the room became brighter and made it possible to distinguish the different objects.

"*Mon Dieu!*" I cried suddenly.

"What's the matter?" Monsieur de Villenave asked, as he lighted the candle.

"*Mon Dieu!* your lovely pastel! What in heaven's name has happened to it?"

"You see," replied Monsieur de Villenave, sadly, "I have put it there by the chimney. I am expecting the picture-framer and the glazier."

"True, the frame is broken, and the glass shattered into a thousand pieces."

"Yes," said Monsieur de Villenave, looking at the portrait with a melancholy air, and forgetting his letter. "Yes, it's an incomprehensible thing."

"Why, did some accident happen to it?"

" Day before yesterday I had worked all the evening. It was about a quarter to twelve. I went to bed, placed my candle on my night table, and was preparing to look over the proofs of a small compact edition of my Ovid, when I chanced to cast my eyes on my poor friend's portrait. I nodded a good-night to her as usual. The wind was blowing gently through the window, which had been left open, and it made the flame of my candle flicker so that it seemed to me that the portrait answered good-night, with a nod like my own. You will understand that I treated the vision as mere folly, but I don't know how it happened. My mind was filled with the idea, and I could not take my eyes off the picture. *Dame !* my friend, that pastel, as you know, dates back to my earliest youth. It recalls all sorts of memories. Imagine me, therefore, swimming in a full flood of reminiscences of the past twenty-five years. I spoke to my portrait. My memory answered for it, and, although it was my memory that answered, it seemed to me that the drawing moved its lips. It seemed to me that its colors faded. It seemed to me that its features assumed a sad expression. At that moment the clock on the Carmelite church began to strike twelve. At the lugubrious sound my poor friend's face assumed a more and more sorrowful expression. The wind continued to blow. At the last stroke of midnight the window of the closet blew open violently. I heard something like a wailing cry, and it seemed to me that the eyes of the portrait closed. The nail on which it hung broke. The portrait fell, and my candle went out.

" I rose to relight it, having no feeling of fear, but deeply impressed, nevertheless. As ill-luck would have it. I could not find a match. It was too late to call, and I did not know where to look for one. I closed the window of the closet and went to bed without a light.

"All this had moved and saddened me. I felt an irresistible longing to weep. It seemed as if I could hear something like the rustling of a silk dress in the room. Several times I said: 'Is there any one here?' At last I fell asleep, but it was quite late, and when I woke I found my poor picture in the condition in which you see it."

"What a strange thing!" I said. "Have you received your weekly letter?"

"What letter?"

"The one that the original of the portrait always writes you."

"No, and that is what worries me. That is why I told Françoise to bring or send up without delay any letters which might come for me."

"Well, this one that I have brought you —"

"It is n't her way of folding her letters."

"Ah!"

"But no matter, it 's from Angers."

"Did she live at Angers?"

"Yes. Ah! my God! sealed with black! Poor, dear friend, can anything have happened to her?"

And Monsieur de Villenave turned pale as he broke the seal.

At the first words he read, his eyes filled with tears.

He took out a second letter, broken off at the fourth line, which was enclosed in the other.

He put the unfinished letter to his lips and handed me the other.

"Read," he said.

I read: —

"MONSIEUR, — My own sorrow is increased by that which you will feel when I inform you that Madame —— died on Sunday last on the last stroke of midnight.

"On the day before, while she was writing to you, she was taken ill with what we thought at first was a slight indisposition only, but she grew rapidly worse until she died.

"I have the honor to send you, incomplete as it is, the letter she had begun for you. That letter will prove to you that, down to the moment of her death, her feeling for you remained the same.

"I am, monsieur, very sadly, as you can believe, but always your very humble servant,

"THÉRÈSE MIRAND."

Monsieur de Villenave followed my eyes as they read the letter.

"At midnight!" he said. "It was at midnight, you remember, that the portrait fell to the floor and was shattered. The coincidence extends not only to the day, but to the hour."

"Yes," I replied. "That is so."

"You believe, then?" cried Monsieur de Villenave.

"Why, of course I believe."

"Oh, then come here some day, my friend, some day when I am a little less disturbed, won't you, and I will tell you something much stranger than that."

"Something that happened to you?"

"No, but something that I saw."

"When was that?"

"Oh, a long time ago. It was in 1774, when I was tutor to Monsieur de Chauvelin's children."

"And you say you will tell it to me?"

"Yes, I will tell you the story. Meanwhile, you understand — "

"I understand. You would like to be alone."

I rose and prepared to go.

3

"By the way," said Monsieur de Villenave, "just tell the ladies, as you go by, not to be disturbed about me. I shall not go down to dinner."

I signified that the errand should be done.

Thereupon Monsieur de Villenave twisted his chair around on one of its hind legs until he faced the portrait; and, as I closed the door, I heard him mutter, —

"Poor Sophie!"

The story you are about to read is the one that Monsieur de Villenave told me later.

IV.

THE KING'S PHYSICIAN.

On the 25th of April, 1774, King Louis XV. was in bed in the Blue Chamber at Versailles. Beside his bed, on a low cot, his physician Lamartinière was sleeping.

The clock in the principal courtyard of the château was striking five.

Shadows flitted restlessly about, careful not to disturb the slumbers of the prince at that hour, at which, for some time past, Louis XV., worn out by late hours and dissipation, had succeeded in obtaining a little rest, purchased by the misuse of insomnia, and by narcotics when that proved insufficient.

The king was no longer young. He was entering his sixty-fifth year. Having drained the cup of pleasure, of dissipation, of flattery to the dregs, there was nothing more for him to learn. He was bored.

The fever of ennui was the worst of his diseases. Acute under Madame de Châteauroux, it had become intermittent under Madame de Pompadour, and chronic under Madame du Barry.

They who have nothing left to learn sometimes have something left to love. That is a sovereign resource against the disease by which Louis XV. was attacked. Satiated in the matter of individual love by that which he had inspired in a whole people, and which had been carried to the point of frenzy, that habit of the heart

had seemed to him too commonplace for a king of France
to indulge in it.

Thus Louis XV. had been beloved by his people, by
his wife, and by his mistresses; but Louis XV. had
never loved any one.

There also remains to those who are blasé another
interesting source of preoccupation, — suffering.   Apart
from the two or three sicknesses he had had, Louis XV.
had never suffered; and, being a highly-favored mortal,
he felt no other warning of the approach of old age
than a beginning of fatigue, which the physicians put
forward as a signal for him to change his ways.

Sometimes, at those famous supper-parties at Choisy,
at which the tables came up, all laden, through the
floor, at which the service was performed by pages from
the *petites écuries*, when the Comtesse du Barry incited
Louis XV. to drink bumper upon bumper, the Duc
d'Ayen to loud laughter, and the Marquis de Chauvelin
to epicurean joviality, Louis XV. observed with surprise that his hand was slow to raise the glass, brim-
ming with the sparkling fluid he had loved so much,
that his brow refused to contract in that inextinguish-
able laughter which Jeanne Vaubernier's sallies had
sometimes caused to bloom on the boundary line of his
ripening years, and that his brain remained cold and
unmoved by the seductive pictures of that blissful life
which sovereign power, supreme wealth, and robust
health afford.

Louis XV. was not naturally open and unreserved.
He concealed his joy and sadness alike.   Perhaps, by
virtue of that inward absorption of his sentiments, he
would have been a great politician, if, as he himself
said, he had not lacked time.

As soon as he noticed the change that was beginning

to take place in him, instead of making the best of it and inhaling philosophically the first breezes of old age, which wrinkle the forehead and silver the hair, he drew back within himself and watched.

The thing that makes the most light-hearted men melancholy is analysis of joy or suffering. Analysis is a period of silence interjected between laughter and sobbing.

Hitherto the courtiers had only seen that the king was bored. Now they saw that he was depressed. He no longer laughed at Madame du Barry's ribald jests; he no longer smiled at the malicious remarks of the Duc d'Ayen; he no longer enjoyed the friendly caresses of Monsieur de Chauvelin, the friend of his heart, the fidus Achates of his royal escapades.

Madame du Barry was loudest in her complaints of this melancholy, whose most noticeable effect was coldness to her.

This moral change caused the doctors to declare that, although the king was not yet sick, he certainly would be before long.

And so, on the 15th of the preceding April, Lamartinière, his first surgeon, after administering to the king his monthly medicine, ventured to make certain suggestions which he considered of grave importance.

" Sire," Lamartinière had said to him, " as Your Majesty has ceased to drink, as Your Majesty has ceased to eat, as Your Majesty has ceased to — amuse yourself, what does Your Majesty propose to do ? "

" *Dame !* my dear Lamartinière," the king replied, " whatever seems most entertaining to me outside of the things you have mentioned."

" The fact is that I do not know much of anything new to suggest to Your Majesty. Your Majesty has been to war, Your Majesty has tried to love scholars and artists, Your Majesty has loved women and champagne. Now, when one has tasted glory, flattery, love, and wine, I declare to Your Majesty that I seek in vain a muscle, a chord, a nerve centre that discloses the existence of any untried aptitude for new forms of distraction."

"Aha!" said the king. "Do you really think so, Lamartinière?"

"Remember, sire, that Sardanapalus was a very intelligent king, almost as intelligent as Your Majesty, although he lived something like twenty-eight hundred years before you. He was fond of life, and devoted much thought to making a good use of it. I think I have read that he paid the most careful attention to the different methods of exercising the body and the mind in the search for little known pleasures. Even so, no historian has ever stated, so far as I know, that he found anything more than you have found yourself."

"Indeed, Lamartinière."

"I except champagne, sire, which Sardanapalus did not know. On the contrary, he had naught to drink but the thick, heavy, heady wines of Asia Minor, those liquid flames which filter through the pulp of the grapes of the archipelago, — wines whose intoxication is a frenzy, while that caused by champagne is only folly."

"True, my dear Lamartinière, true. Champagne is a pretty little wine, and I have been very fond of it. But tell me, did n't your Sardanapalus end by being burned at the stake?"

"Yes, sire, that was the only variety of pleasure that he had never tried. He kept it for the last."

"And it was with a view of making that pleasure as

intense as possible, I doubt not, that he burned up his palace, his wealth, and his favorite with himself?"

"Yes, sire."

"And would you advise me, my dear Lamartinière, to burn Versailles, and to burn myself and Madame du Barry at the same time?"

"No, sire. You have made war; you have seen conflagrations; you have been yourself in the thick of the cannonade at Fontenoy. Consequently fire would not be a novel form of entertainment to you. Come, let us recapitulate your means of defence against ennui."

"O Lamartinière, I am almost defenceless."

"In the first place, you have your friend, Monsieur de Chauvelin, a man of wit, a — "

"Chauvelin is no longer a man of wit, my dear fellow."

"Since when?"

"*Pardieu!* since I have been bored."

"Bah!" said Lamartinière. "That's as if you should say that Madame du Barry has ceased to be beautiful since — "

"Since what?" said the king, blushing a little.

"Oh! I know what I know," rejoined the surgeon brusquely.

"Well," said the king with a sigh, "it seems to be settled that I am going to be sick."

"I am afraid so, sire."

"Give me a remedy, then, Lamartinière, a remedy. Let us get the start of the disease."

"Rest, sire. I know no other."

"Very good!"

"Diet."

"Very good!"

" Amusement."

" I stop you there, Lamartinière."

" Why so ? "

" You prescribe amusement and you don't tell me how I am to amuse myself. Very good! I consider you an ignoramus, an *ignorantissimus*, my friend! Do you hear ? "

" And you are wrong, sire. It is your fault, not mine."

" How so ? "

" It is a hopeless task to amuse those who are bored when they have such a friend as Monsieur de Chauvelin and such a mistress as Madame du Barry."

There was a pause, which seemed to indicate that the king acknowledged that what Lamartinière had said was not altogether devoid of sense.

Then the king continued, —

" Well, Lamartinière, my friend, as we are talking of diseases, let us reason together. You say that I have amused myself with everything in this world capable of furnishing amusement, do you not ? "

" I say so, and it is so."

" With war ? "

" *Pardieu !* I should say so, when you have won the battle of Fontenoy ! "

" Yes, and it was a diverting spectacle too, — men in rags, and a tract four leagues long and one league wide soaked with blood; a smell of the shambles to do your heart good."

" And the glory, too ! "

" But, after all, did I win the battle ? Was n't it Monsieur le Maréchal de Saxe ? Was n't it Monsieur le Duc de Richelieu ? Was n't it Pecquigny more than all the rest, with his four guns ? "

"Never mind. Who gets all the credit of it? You."

"I believe you; and so that is the reason why you imagine that I must love glory. Ah! my dear Lamartinière," the king added, heaving a sigh, " if you knew what a wretched bed I slept on the night before Fontenoy! "

"Oh, well! Let us leave glory out of the question. If you don't choose to acquire it yourself, you can let the painters, poets, and historians make it for you."

"Lamartinière, I have a perfect horror of all those people, who are either pitiful creatures, duller than my lackeys, or giants of pride too tall to pass under my great-grandfather's triumphal arches. That Voltaire above all. Why, did not the knave lay his hand on my shoulder one evening and call me Trajan? People tell him that he is the king of my kingdom, and the puppy believes it. So I don't want any of the immortality those people could give me. One has to pay too high a price for it in this perishable world, and perhaps in the other too."

"In that case, what do you want, sire? Tell me."

"I want to make my life last as long as possible. I want to have in my life the greatest possible number of things I love; and for that I shall not apply to poets or philosophers or warriors. No, Lamartinière, except God, I really have no esteem for anybody but the doctors, — when they are good ones, I mean, of course."

" *Parbleu !* "

" So speak frankly, my dear Lamartinière."

" Yes, sire."

" What have I to dread? "

" Apoplexy."

" Do people die of it? "

"Yes, if they are not bled in time."

"Lamartinière, you must not leave me any more."

"That is impossible, sire. I have my other patients."

"Indeed! but it seems to me that my health is a matter of as much interest to France and to Europe as that of all your patients together. A bed will be made up for you beside mine every night."

"Sire!"

"What difference does it make to you whether you sleep here or elsewhere? And you will reassure me by your mere presence, Lamartinière, and you will frighten away disease, for disease knows you and knows that it has no sturdier foe than you."

That is why Lamartinière was lying in a low bed in the Blue Chamber at Versailles on April 25, 1774, sleeping soundly, about five o'clock in the morning, while the king was wide awake.

Louis XV., who, as we have stated, was not asleep, heaved a great sigh; but, inasmuch as a sigh has no positive meaning except that which the sigher gives to it, Lamartinière, who was snoring instead of sighing, heard it as he snored, but paid, or rather seemed to pay, no attention to it.

The king, seeing that his surgeon in ordinary was insensible to that appeal, leaned over the edge of the bed, and, by the light of the great candle burning in the marble candlestick, he gazed at the form of his watcher, who was hidden from the most persistent gaze by the thick, soft coverlid that reached to the topknot of his nightcap.

"Ah!" said the king, "alas!" Lamartinière heard him; but as an interjection may sometimes escape a sleeping man, there is no reason why it should wake another.

So the surgeon continued to snore.

"How lucky he is to be able to sleep like that!" muttered Louis XV. "What material creatures these doctors are!"

And he resigned himself to wait still longer; but, after waiting in vain for a quarter of an hour, he called, —

"Hé! Lamartinière!"

"What is it, sire?" growled His Majesty's adviser.

"Oh! my poor Lamartinière!" said the king, groaning as piteously as he could.

"Well! what is it?"

And the doctor, still grumbling like a man who is sure that he can safely presume upon his position, slipped out of bed.

He found the king sitting up in bed.

"Are you in pain, sire?" he asked.

"I think so, my dear Lamartinière," His Majesty replied.

"Oho! you are slightly excited."

"Very much excited, yes."

"At what?"

"I have no idea."

"I know," muttered the surgeon; "it's fear."

"Feel my pulse, Lamartinière."

"That's what I am doing."

"How is it?"

"It marks eighty-eight pulsations a minute, sire, and that is a good many in an old man."

"In an old man, Lamartinière?"

"To be sure."

"I am only sixty-four, and at sixty-four a man's not old."

"He is no longer young, certainly."

"Well, what do you prescribe?"

"First of all, how do you feel?"

"It seems to me that I am stifling with the heat."

"On the contrary, you are cold."

"I must be flushed, am I not?"

"Nonsense, you are pale. Let me give you some advice, sire."

"What is it?"

"Try to go to sleep again; that would be the proper thing."

"I am no longer sleepy."

"What is the meaning of this excitement?"

"*Dame!* it seems to me that you ought to know, Lamartinière, or else it is hardly worth while to be a doctor."

"Have you had a bad dream?"

"Well, yes, I have."

"A dream!" cried Lamartinière, throwing up his hands; "a dream!"

"*Dame!*" rejoined the king. "There are such things as dreams."

"Very good! come, tell me your dream, sire."

"That's one of the things that isn't told, my friend."

"Why so? People tell everything."

"To their confessors, yes."

"Then send me for your confessor at once; and I'll bring my lancet too."

"A dream is sometimes a secret."

"Yes, and sometimes it's caused by remorse. You are right, sire; adieu."

And the doctor began to pull on his stockings and his breeches.

"Come, come, Lamartinière, don't be angry, my

friend. Well! I dreamed — I dreamed that I was being carried to Saint-Denis."

"And that it was an uncomfortable carriage. Bah! when you take that trip, you won't notice the carriage, sire."

"How can you joke on such subjects?" said the king, shuddering from head to foot. "No, I dreamed that I was being carried to Saint-Denis, and that I was confined alive in the velvet lining of my coffin."

"You felt uncomfortable in the coffin?"

"Yes, a little."

"Vapors, bile, sluggish digestion."

"Oh! I didn't sup yesterday."

"An empty stomach then."

"Do you think so?"

"Ah! now I think of it, at what time did you leave Madame la Comtesse yesterday?"

"I haven't seen her for two days."

"You are sulking, eh? Bile, you see."

"No, no! she is sulking with me. I promised her something that I haven't given her."

"Give her that something quickly, and recover your good spirits."

"No, I am drowned in melancholy."

"Ah! I have an idea."

"What is it?"

"Breakfast with Monsieur de Chauvelin."

"Breakfast!" cried the king. "That was a very good thing to do in the days when I had an appetite."

"Bless my soul!" cried the surgeon, folding his arms. "You will have none of your mistress; you'll have none of your friends; you'll have none of your breakfast. And you imagine that I'll allow that, do you? Well, sire, I tell you one thing, and that is that, if you change your habits, you are a doomed man."

"My friend makes me yawn, Lamartinière; my mistress puts me to sleep; my breakfast chokes me."

"The deuce! decidedly, you must be sick then."

"Ah! Lamartinière," cried the king, "I was happy a long while."

"And you complain of that? That is human gratitude."

"No, I don't complain of the past, certainly not, but of the present. The carriage wears out by use."

And the king heaved a sigh.

"True, it does wear out," the surgeon repeated sententiously.

"So that the springs refuse to work," sighed the king; "and I long for repose."

"Well, go to sleep, then!" cried Lamartinière, going back to bed.

"Let me go on with my metaphor, my dear doctor."

"Can I be mistaken, and are you turning poet, sire? Another villainous disease that!"

"No; on the contrary, you know that I detest poets. To please Madame de Pompadour I made that wretch Voltaire a gentleman; but on the day when he presumed to thee-and-thou me and call me Titus or Trajan, I put a stop to that sort of thing. I intended to say, without poetry, that I think it is time for me to put on the drag."

"Do you wish to know my opinion, sire?"

"Yes, my friend."

"Well then, don't put on the drag, but unharness the horses."

"That's a harsh remedy," murmured Louis XV.

"It is the only true one, sire. When I address the

king I call him Your Majesty. When I turn over my patient I don't even call him monsieur. Unharness, therefore, sire, and at once. Now that the matter is decided, we still have an hour and a half to sleep, sire, so let us sleep."

The surgeon drew the coverlid over him once more, and five minutes later was snoring in such plebeian fashion that the walls of the Blue Chamber gnashed their teeth with indignation.

V.

THE KING'S MORNING RECEPTION.

THE king, left to himself, did not attempt to disturb the obstinate doctor, whose slumber, being as well regulated as a clock, lasted just as long as he had announced.

The clock had struck half-past six. As the valet de chambre entered the room, Lamartinière rose and went into an adjoining closet while his bed was being removed.

There he wrote a prescription for the physicians on duty for the day, and disappeared.

The king ordered that his regular attendants should be admitted first and then those who had the *grandes entrées*.

He saluted silently, then gave his legs to the valets de chambre, who drew on his stockings, fastened his garters, and arrayed him in his dressing-gown.

Then he knelt before his prie-Dieu, sighing several times amid the general silence.

Every one had knelt with the king and prayed as he was doing, thinking of other things.

The king turned from time to time toward the balustrade where the most intimate and most favored of his courtiers were ordinarily assembled.

"Whom is the king looking for?" the Duc de Richelieu and the Duc d'Ayen asked each other in an undertone.

"Not for us, for he would find us," said the Duc d'Ayen; "but see, the king is rising!"

Louis XV. had, in fact, finished his prayer, or had been so distraught, rather, that he had not said it.

"I do not see monsieur the keeper of the wardrobe," said Louis XV., casting his eyes about.

"Monsieur de Chauvelin?" asked the Duc de Richelieu.

"Yes."

"But he is here, sire."

"Where, pray?"

"There," said the duke, turning round. "Aha!" he added suddenly, as if in surprise.

"What is it?" demanded the king.

"Monsieur de Chauvelin is still praying."

In truth the Marquis de Chauvelin, that entertaining heathen, that jovial accomplice in the petty royal sacrileges, that witty adversary of the gods in general and of God in particular, had remained on his knees, not only contrary to his usual custom, but also, contrary to etiquette, the king having finished his prayer.

"Well, marquis," queried the king with a smile, "are you asleep?"

The marquis rose slowly to his feet, crossed himself, and saluted Louis XV. with profound respect.

Every one was in the habit of laughing when Monsieur de Chauvelin chose to laugh; they supposed that he was joking and laughed from force of habit, the king with the rest. But he resumed his serious demeanor almost immediately.

"Come, come, marquis," he said, "you know that I am not fond of jesting on sacred subjects. However, as I presume that you wish to cheer me up a little, I forgive you because of the intention; but I warn you that you have a hard task," he added with a sigh, "for I am as depressed as death."

4

"You are depressed, sire?" said the Duc d'Ayen. "I pray to know what can have happened to depress Your Majesty?"

"My health, duke! my health, which is failing me! I make Lamartinière sleep in my bedroom to encourage me; but the fiend makes it his business to frighten me instead. Luckily every one seems inclined to laugh here. Isn't that so, Chauvelin?"

But the king's lures produced no result. The Marquis de Chauvelin himself, whose intelligent, mocking features were usually so quick to reflect the master's playful mood, who was so perfect a courtier that he never failed to respond to a desire on the king's part, on this occasion, instead of responding to Louis XV.'s expressed craving for even a trifling distraction, remained gloomy and severe, entirely absorbed by inexplicable gravity.

Some of those present — such gloom was so foreign to all Monsieur de Chauvelin's ways — some, we say, believed that the marquis was keeping up the jest, and that his gravity would end in a gorgeous display of hilarity. But the king had not the patience to wait that morning; he began therefore a determined assault upon his friend's melancholy.

"Why, what in the devil is the matter with you, Chauvelin?" he demanded; "are you going on with my dream of last night? Do you also propose to have yourself buried alive?"

"Oh! oh! has Your Majesty been dreaming about such villainous things as that?" asked Richelieu.

"Yes, I had the nightmare, duke. But, upon my word, I should be very glad not to find, when I wake, a state of things that I can endure when I am asleep. Come! Chauvelin, tell me what's the matter with you?"

The marquis bowed without replying.

"Speak, speak, I tell you; I insist upon it!" cried the king.

"Sire," replied the marquis, "I am reflecting."

"Reflecting about what?" demanded Louis in amazement.

"God, sire!"

"God?"

"Yes, sire. God — is the beginning of wisdom."

That cold, monkish preamble made the king start; and, upon looking more attentively at the marquis, he detected in his worn, haggard features the probable explanation of his unaccustomed depression.

"The beginning of wisdom?" he said. "Ah! indeed, I shall not be surprised if that beginning never has any sequel; it's too tiresome. But you were not reflecting about God all by himself. What else were you reflecting about?"

"My wife and children, whom I have not seen for a long while, sire."

"True, true, Chauvelin; you are married and have children. 1 had forgotten it, and so had you, too, 1 should say, for this is the first time you have ever mentioned it during these fifteen years that we have seen each other every day. Oh, well! if you have a fancy to see the domestic kettle boil, send for them; I've no objection. Your apartments at the château are large enough, I imagine."

"Sire," replied the marquis, "Madame de Chauvelin lives in strict retirement, devoted to the duties of religion, and — "

"And she would be scandalized, eh, by the goings on at Versailles? I understand. She is like my daughter Louise, whom I cannot induce to leave Saint-

Denis. In that case I can see no remedy, my dear marquis."

"I ask the king's pardon; there is one."

"What is that?"

"My term of service ends this evening. If the king would permit me to go to Grosbois to pass a few days with my family — "

"You are jesting, marquis; leave me?"

"I will return, sire; but I should not like to die without having made some testamentary arrangements."

"Die! what a devil of a man! Die! how he says it! How old are you, marquis, pray?"

"Ten years younger than your majesty, sire, although I seem to be ten years older."

The king turned his back on the humorist, and turned to the Duc de Coigny, who was standing very near his raised platform.

"Ah! there you are, Monsieur le Duc," he said. "You come most opportunely; we were speaking of you the other evening at supper. Is it true that you entertained poor Gentil-Bernard in my château of Choisy? That would be a good action for which I should praise you heartily. However, if all the governors of my châteaux did the same, and offered an asylum to poets who had gone mad, there would be no resource left for me but to go and live at Bicêtre. How is the poor fellow?"

"Still very badly off, sire."

"And how did the trouble come upon him?"

'From having amused himself a little too much heretofore, sire, and especially from having very recently tried to play the young man."

"Yes, yes, I understand. *Dame!* he is very old."

"I ask the king's pardon, sire, but he is only a year older than Your Majesty."

"Upon my word, this is beyond endurance," said the king, turning his back on the Duc de Coigny. "Not only are they all as melancholy as catafalques to-day, but they 're as stupid as geese."

The Duc d'Ayen, one of the cleverest men of that clever age, detected the king's increasing ill-humor, and feared that he might be spattered by it; and so, having determined to put an end to it at the earliest possible moment, he stepped forward to attract the king's attention. He wore on his doublet, around his garters, and around the edge of his coat, gold embroidery, so broad and conspicuous that it could not fail to catch the eye. The monarch noticed it.

"By my troth! Duc d'Ayen," he exclaimed, "you are as resplendent as a sun. Have you been robbing a caravan, pray? I thought all the makers of embroidery in Paris were ruined since the marriage of the Comte de Provence, when not a single courtier paid them, and which messieurs the princes did not see fit to attend, for lack of money or of credit, I doubt not."

"And so they are, sire, altogether ruined."

"Who, the princes, the makers of embroidery, or the courtiers?"

"Why, all of them to some extent, I fancy; but the embroidery people are more shrewd, they will come out whole."

"How so?"

"By virtue of this new invention." And he pointed to his own embroideries.

"I don't understand."

"Why, coats embroidered in this way, sire, are called *à la chancelière*."

"I understand still less."

"There is one method of explaining the enigma to

Your Majesty,— to quote the verses that those idiotic Parisians have concocted,— but I don't dare."

"*You* don't dare, duke!" said the king smiling.

"Faith! no, sire; I await the king's order."

"I give you the order."

"The king will remember, of course, that I am simply obeying orders. These are the verses:—

" 'On fait certain galons de nouvelle matière;
    Mais ils ne sont que pour jours de galas,
    On les nomme à la chancelière.
  Pourquoi?   C'est qu'ils sont faux et ne rougissent pas.' " [1]

The courtiers exchanged glances, amazed at such excessive audacity, and all turned at the same moment toward Louis XV., in order to model their faces upon his. The Chancellor Maupeou, then in high favor, being supported by the favorite, was so exalted a personage that no one dared listen to the epigrams against him which succeeded one another in an endless stream. The monarch smiled, and immediately every mouth was wreathed in smiles. He made no reply, so no one said a word.

Louis XV. had a strange temperament. He was horribly afraid of death, and he did not wish anybody to mention his death to him. But on every occasion he took a sort of delight in laughing at the tendency that almost all men exhibit to conceal their age or their infirmities. He delighted to say to a courtier,—

"You are an old man, you don't look well, you will die soon."

---

[1] They are making gold lace of a new material;
    But it is for use only on gala days.
    It is called lace *à la chancelière*.[1]
  Why?   Because it is false and does not blush.

      [1] *Chancelière.*— the chancellor's wife.

He was philosophical withal, and on that very day on which he had twice received cruel thrusts, he exposed himself to the risk of a third.

To resume his interrupted conversation with the Duc d'Ayen, he said to him abruptly, —

"How is the Chevalier de Noailles? Is it true that he is ill?"

"We had the misfortune to lose him yesterday, sire."

"Ah! I told him it was coming."

Then, glancing around the circle of courtiers, now increased by those who had the *petites entrées*, he noticed the Abbé de Broglio, a man of a surly disposition and brusque manners. He addressed him thus: —

"It's your turn next, abbé. You are just two days younger than he."

"Sire," retorted Monsieur de Broglio, white with rage, "Your Majesty hunted yesterday. A storm came up. The king got wet like the rest."

He made a path for himself through the throng, and left the room in a towering passion.

The king looked after him with a melancholy expression, and remarked, —

"That is the way that Abbé de Broglio always acts; he loses his temper continually."

Then, noticing his physician Bonnard at the door, and with him Bordeu, a protégé of Madame du Barry, who aspired to take his place, he called them both.

"Come, messieurs; the talk is all of death here this morning, and that interests you. Which of you will find the fountain of Jouvence for us? That would be a marvel indeed, and would assure his fortune, I will answer for it. Are you the man, Bordeu? I can understand that you, Æsculapius in attendance upon Venus, have not as yet had occasion to think about patching and repairing the human frame."

"I ask the king's pardon, but I have, on the contrary, a system which should take us back to those halycon days."

"Of fable!" interrupted Bonnard, with an expression of disgust.

"Do you think so," said the king, "do you think so, my poor Bonnard? The fact is that, under your guidance, my youth is no longer anything but a very unpalatable fable, and the man who should give me back my youth would be historiographer of France by the same token; for he would have written the fairest pages of my reign. Make it a cure deserving of the greatest celebrity, Bordeu. Meanwhile, feel Monsieur de Chauvelin's pulse, for he is pale and depressed. Give me your opinion as to his health, which is most precious to our enjoyment — and to my heart," he added hastily.

Chauvelin smiled bitterly as he bared his wrist for the doctor.

"Which of you two, messieurs?" he asked.

"Let both of them feel it," laughed Louis XV., "but not Lamartinière. He is just the man to predict apoplexy, as he did to me."

"Very good, you, Monsieur Bonnard; the past before the future. What is your opinion?"

"Monsieur le marquis is very ill; the blood-vessels of the brain are full and obstructed; he would do well to be bled, and that very soon."

"And you, Monsieur Bordeu?"

"I beg my learned confrère to excuse me; but I am obliged to differ from his experience. Monsieur le marquis has a nervous pulse. If I were talking to a pretty woman, I should say that she had the vapors. He needs cheerful scenes, repose, no worry, no business cares, complete contentment; in short, everything that he finds at the court of the august monarch, whose friend he has the honor to be. I prescribe a continuation of the same régime."

"There are two valuable opinions, and Monsieur de Chauvelin ought to be thoroughly enlightened by them. My poor marquis, if you die, Bordeu is a disgraced man."

"No, sire, the vapors kill when they are not attended to."

"If I die, sire," replied Monsieur de Chauvelin, "I pray to God that it may be at your feet."

"Do nothing of the sort, you would frighten me terribly. But is n't it the hour for mass? I think I see Monsieur the Bishop of Senez, and Monsieur the Curé of Saint-Louis, our parish. Now, I shall certainly get a little consolation. Good-morning, Monsieur le Curé, how goes your flock? Are there many sick and poor?"

"Alas! sire, there are very many."

"But are not alms abundant? Has the price of bread gone up? Has the number of unfortunates increased?"

"Ah! yes, sire."

"How does it happen? Where do they come from?"

"Sire, even the footmen in your household come to me for charity."

"I can well believe it, for they are not paid. Do you hear, Monsieur de Richelieu? Can you not arrange that? Deuce take it! You are first gentleman-in-waiting for the year."

"Sire, the footmen are not in my department; that is a matter for the intendant-general to attend to."

"And he will send it on to some one else. Poor fellows!" said the king, moved to pity for an instant; "but after all I cannot do everything. Do you go with

us to mass, bishop ? " he added, turning to Abbé de
Beauvais, Bishop of Senez, who was the Lenten preacher
at court.

"I am at Your Majesty's service," replied the bishop
bowing; "but I have listened to words of grave import
here. You talk of death and no one thinks seriously
about it; no one reflects that it comes in its own good
time, when it is not expected, that it comes upon us in
the midst of our pleasures, that it mows down great and
small with its inexorable scythe. No one reflects that
there comes a time of life when repentance and penance
are as much a necessity as a duty, when the fires of con-
cupiscence should die away before the great thought of
salvation."

"Richelieu," the king interrupted with a smile, "it
seems to me that monsieur the bishop is throwing a
good many stones into your garden."

"Yes, sire, and he throws them with such force that
they rebound into the park of Versailles."

"Ah! well answered, Monsieur le Duc; you are still
as quick at repartee as you were at twenty years of age.
The discourse begins well, my dear bishop, and we will
hear the rest of it Sunday, in the chapel. I promise to
listen. Chauvelin, we excuse you from attending us, in
order to brighten you up a bit. Go and wait for me at
the countess'," he added, in an undertone. "She has
received her famous golden mirror, Rotiers' chef-d'œuvre.
You must see it."

"I prefer to go to Grosbois, sire."

"Again! you are in your dotage, my dear fellow; go
and see the countess, she will disenchant you. To mass,
messieurs ! to mass! This day begins very badly. That
is what it is to grow old ! "

VI.

MADAME DU BARRY'S MIRROR.

THE marquis, in order to obey the king's command, betook himself to the favorite's apartments despite his repugnance to do so.

The favorite was in a seventh heaven of delight. She was dancing about like a child, and as soon as Monsieur le Marquis de Chauvelin was announced, she ran to him and cried, without giving him time to speak, —

"Oh, my dear marquis, my dear marquis, you come just in the nick of time! I am the happiest woman in the world to-day! I had the most delightful waking you can imagine! In the first place Rotiers sent me my mirror. That 's what you came to see, of course; but we must wait for the king. And then, as good luck always comes in showers, the famous carriage has arrived, the carriage Monsieur d'Aiguillon has given me, you know."

"Oh, yes," said the marquis. "The *vis-à-vis* everybody is talking about. He owed you that, madame."

"Oh! I know that people are talking about it. *Mon Dieu!* I even know what they say about it."

"Really, do you know everything?"

"Yes, almost; but I snap my fingers at it, you understand! Look, here are some verses I found this very morning in the pockets of the *vis-à-vis*. I might

have the poor saddler arrested, but pshaw! That sort
of thing was all right for Madame de Pompadour. I
am too well pleased to think about revenge. Besides,
it seems to me that the verses are n't bad, and if they
would always treat me so, on my word of honor, I
would n't complain."

And she handed the verses to Monsieur de Chauvelin.

Monsieur de Chauvelin took them and read them: —

> "Pourquoi ce brillant vis-à-vis ?
> Est-ce le char d'une déesse
> Ou de quelque jeune princesse ?
> S'écriait un badaud surpris.
> Non — de la foule curieuse
> Lui répond un caustique, non,
> C'est le char de la blanchisseuse,
> De cet infâme D'Aiguillon ! " [1]

And the reckless courtesan roared with laughter.
Then she continued: —

"*Of that infamous D'Aiguillon*, you see, *his
laundress*. Ah! on my word, the author is right, and
he does n't say too much. Except for me, in truth,
the poor duke, notwithstanding the flour he covered
himself with at the battle of — I never can remember
the names of battles — except for me, the poor duke
would still be frightfully black. But pshaw! What
does it matter, as my predecessor, Monsieur de Mazarin,

---

[1] " Why this gorgeous *vis-à-vis* ?
Is it some goddess' chariot,
Or that of a fair young princess ? "
Cried a gaping, wondering lout.
" No " — from the throng of curious bystanders
A caustic wit made answer — " no,
'T is the chariot of the laundress
Of that infamous D'Aiguillon ! "

used to say, *they sing and they pay ;* and a single
panel of my *vis-à-vis* is worth more than all the
epigrams against me that have been made in four
years. I will show it to you. Come, marquis, follow me."

And the countess, forgetting that she was no longer
Jeanne Vaubernier, and forgetting the marquis' age,
tripped singing down the steps of a secret staircase
leading to a small courtyard where the carriage-houses
were.

"Look," she said to the marquis, who was panting
for breath, " is that very bad for a laundress' carriage ? "

The marquis was speechless. Nothing more mag-
nificent and more refined at once had ever met his gaze.
On the four principal panels were the arms of the Du
Barrys, with the famous war-cry, *Boute en avant.*

Upon each of the side-panels was a basket of roses on
which two doves were tenderly pecking at each other,
the whole varnished with the Martin varnish, the
secret of which is lost now.

The carriage cost fifty-six thousand francs.

"Has the king seen the superb gift, Madame la
Comtesse ? " asked the Marquis de Chauvelin.

"Not yet, but I am sure of one thing."

"Of what are you sure ? let us hear."

"That he will be charmed with it."

"Oho! "

"Why that oho ? "

"Because I doubt it."

"You doubt it ? "

"I will even go so far as to bet that he will not
allow you to accept it."

"Why not ? "

"Because you could not use it."

"Oh! indeed?" she retorted ironically. "Are you astonished by such a small matter?"

"Yes."

"You shall see something very different then; both the golden mirror and this," she added, taking a paper from her pocket. "But no, you sha'n't see this."

"As you please, madame," rejoined the marquis bowing.

"However, you're the king's oldest friend, next to that old monkey of a Richelieu. You know him well. He listens to you. You could help me, if you chose, and in that case — come up to my closet again, marquis."

"At your service, madame."

"You are very disagreeable to-day. Pray, what is the matter with you?"

"I am sad, madame."

"Ah! so much the worse. That's foolish!"

And Madame du Barry, acting as the marquis' guide, ascended with a more sedate step the secret staircase which she had just descended, light of foot and singing like a bird.

She returned to her closet, Monsieur de Chauvelin still following her. Then she closed the door and said, turning quickly to the marquis, —

"You do not care for me, do you, Chauvelin?"

"You cannot doubt my respect and my devotion, madame."

"Will you serve me against everybody?"

"Against everybody except the king."

"In any event, if you don't approve of what you are going to hear, you will remain neutral."

"I will agree to do so if you demand it."

"Give me your word."

"On the word of Chauvelin!"

" Read then."

And the countess handed him the most extraordinary, most audacious, most ridiculous composition that ever was placed before the eyes of a gentleman. The marquis did not understand at first its full scope.

It was a petition addressed to the pope for the annulment of her marriage to Comte du Barry, on the pretext that, as she had been his brother's mistress, and as any sort of alliance was forbidden by the canons under such circumstances, the marriage was necessarily void. She added that, having been informed immediately after the ceremony was performed of the sacrilege she was on the point of committing, of which she had had no suspicion before, she had been stricken with fear, and the marriage had not been consummated.

The marquis read the petition twice over, then handed it back to the countess, and asked her what she intended to do with it.

" Why, send it, of course," she replied with her usual effrontery.

" To whom? "

" To its address."

" To the pope? "

" To the pope."

" And then? "

" You cannot guess? "

" No."

" Great heaven! how hard your head is to-day! "

" That may be; but it's a fact that I cannot guess."

" Did you think, pray, that I had no object in patronizing Madame de Montesson? Have you forgotten the grand dauphin and Mademoiselle Choin, Louis XIV. and Madame de Maintenon? People are crying to the king all day to imitate his illustrious

ancestor. After this they'll have nothing to say.
I'm as good as the Widow Scarron, I imagine; and
I'm not sixty years old into the bargain."

"O madame, madame! what do I hear?" exclaimed
Monsieur de Chauvelin, turning pale and stepping back.

At that moment the door opened and Zamore
announced, —

"The king!"

"The king!" cried Madame du Barry, seizing
Monsieur de Chauvelin's hand; "the king! not a
word. We will continue this subject another time."

The king entered.

His eyes rested first on Madame du Barry, and yet he
spoke first to the marquis.

"Ah! Chauvelin! Chauvelin!" he cried, impressed
by the agitation visible on the marquis' features, "do
you really propose to die for good and all? Upon my
word you look like a ghost, my friend."

"Die! Monsieur de Chauvelin die!" laughed the
heedless young woman. "Oh, no! I forbid him to do
it. In heaven's name, sire, do you forget the horoscope that was cast for him five years ago at the fair of
the Loges de Saint-Germain?"

"What horoscope?" the king asked.

"Must I repeat it?"

"Certainly."

"You don't believe in horoscopes, I trust, sire."

"No, but tell it all the same, whether I believe in
them or not."

"Well, some one predicted that Monsieur de
Chauvelin would die two months before Your
Majesty."

"Who was the fool who predicted that?" queried
the king with some uneasiness.

" A very clever sorcerer, the same who told me — "

" That is all nonsense," interrupted the king with well-marked impatience. " Let us see the mirror."

" In that case, sire, we must go into the adjoining room."

" Let us go there."

" Show us the way, sire. You know it. It is your very humble servant's bedroom." The king did in fact know the way, and he went first.

The mirror was on the toilet table, covered with a thick veil, which fell at a word from the king, disclosing a veritable masterpiece worthy of Benvenuto Cellini. The mirror, in a solid gold frame, was surmounted by two Cupids in relief, holding a royal crown, beneath which the head of the person who happened to be looking into the mirror naturally took its place.

" Ah! that's a magnificent thing! " cried the king. " Really, Rotiers has surpassed himself. I will congratulate him. Countess, I give you this, you understand."

" You give me the whole thing? "

" Of course."

" Mirror and frame? "

" Mirror and frame."

" Including that? " added the countess with a siren's smile that staggered the marquis, especially after what he had just read, for she was pointing to the royal crown.

" That plaything? " said the king.

The countess nodded.

" Oh! you can amuse yourself with that as much as you please, countess; but, I give you fair warning, it is heavy. Come, come, Chauvelin, won't you smoooth out your wrinkles even in madame's presence, and in presence of her mirror, which is a double favor she accords you, as in that way you see her twice ? "

The royal flattery was rewarded by a kiss from the countess.

The marquis did not relax.

" What do you think of the mirror, marquis ?   Come, tell us your opinion."

" For what purpose, sire ? "

" Why, because you are a man of good taste, *pardieu !* "

" I should have preferred not to see it."

" Bah! why so ? "

" Because then I could at least have denied its existence."

" What does that mean ? "

" Sire, the royal crown is ill-placed in the hands of Cupids," replied the marquis, bowing low.

Madame du Barry became purple with wrath.

The king, deeply embarrassed, tried to look as if he did not understand.

" Why, on the contrary, those Cupids are lovely," he rejoined.   " They hold the crown with such grace as never was seen.   Look at their little arms, how gracefully rounded they are.   Would not one say they were carrying a garland of flowers ? "

" That is their proper employment, sire.   Cupids are good for nothing else."

" Cupids are good for everything, Monsieur de Chauvelin," said the countess.   " You used not to doubt it; but at your age a man forgets such things."

" To be sure, and it is proper for young people like me to remember them," laughed the king.   " So the mirror does not please you ? "

" It is not the mirror, sire."

" What in heaven's name is it then ?   Can it be the

charming face that is reflected in it? The devil! you are hard to please, marquis."

"On the contrary, no one pays more sincere homage to madame's beauty."

"But," interposed Madame du Barry, testily, "if it's not the mirror nor the face reflected in it, what is it? Tell us."

"It is the position it occupies."

"Why, doesn't it look wonderfully well on this toilet table, which, like it, is a gift from His Majesty?"

"It would look better elsewhere."

"Where, in God's name? For you annoy me with this air that no one ever saw you adopt before."

"In madame la dauphine's apartments, madame."

"What?"

"Yes, the crown with the fleurs-de-lis can be worn only by one who has been, is, or will be queen of France."

Madame du Barry's eyes flashed fire.

The king frowned threateningly.

Then he rose saying, —

"You are right, Marquis de Chauvelin. Your mind is diseased. Go and seek repose at Grosbois, as you are so unhappy with us. Go, marquis, go."

Monsieur de Chauvelin made no other reply than a low bow, and walked backward from the room as he would have done from the state apartments at Versailles; and, mindful of the rigid rule of etiquette that forbids saluting any person whomsoever in the king's presence, he went out without so much as glancing at the countess.

The countess gnawed her nails with rage. The king tried to soothe her.

"Poor Chauvelin!" he said. "He must have had some such dream as I had. In truth all strong minds surrender at the first touch of the black angel's wing. Chauvelin is ten years younger than I, and I still claim to be a better man than he."

"Oh! yes, sire, you are a better man than anybody in the world. You are cleverer than your ministers and younger than your children."

The king beamed at that last compliment, which he did his best to deserve, despite Lamartinière's advice.

VII.

THE MONK, THE TUTOR, THE STEWARD.

On the day following that on which the king had given Monsieur de Chauvelin permission to retire to his estates, the Marquise de Chauvelin was walking in the park at Grosbois with her children and their tutor.

A saint-like, noble woman, left in oblivion in the shade of those great oaks by the corruption that had devoured France for fifty years past, Madame de Chauvelin still retained her hold upon God who blessed her, her children who loved her, and her servants who worshipped her.

She gave God her prayers, returned the love of her children, and was charitable to her neighbor.

Always interested in the pursuits of her husband, she followed him with her thoughts on the tempestuous stage of the court, as the sailor's wife follows with her heart her poor husband wandering amid storm and fog.

The marquis had loved his wife dearly. Having become a courtier and a favorite, he had never hazarded his last stake in the game which kings always win against their favorites, — the joys of domestic life, the last, pure flame upon which he smiled from afar. The seaman of whom we spoke just now kept watch of that family love as the shipwrecked man watches the light-house. He hoped to warm himself after the squall at his own always blazing, always joyous fireside.

It should be said to Monsieur de Chauvelin's credit that he had never compelled the marchioness to come to Versailles to live.

The pious creature would have obeyed. She would have sacrificed herself. But the marquis had never broached the subject to her but once.

At the first sign of regret that appeared in his wife's eyes he said no more. It was not, as evil-minded people said, that Monsieur de Chauvelin was afraid of his wife's sermons. Every rake, every courtier who crawled at the feet of the concubine or the monarch could muster sufficient courage to browbeat his wife and scold his children.

No, Monsieur de Chauvelin had left the marchioness to her devout reflections.

"I am laying up enough acres of land in hell," he said. "I will let the excellent marchioness secure a few inches of azure for me in heaven."

He was hardly even seen at Grosbois. His wife made a holiday for him every year when he arrived at Saint-André.

The programme never varied. Monsieur de Chauvelin kissed his children at two o'clock, dined with his family, entered his carriage at six, and was present at the king's *coucher*.[1]

For four years he had done nothing more than that. In four years he had touched his lips four times to the marchioness' hand. On New Year's Day his sons went to Versailles with their governor to see him.

Monsieur de Chauvelin intrusted his wife with the education of their children. Abbé V——, a scholarly

[1] The *coucher* was the reception held by the king when he retired, as the *lever* was the one attending his rising in the morning.

young man who had not yet received orders, but who was called abbé by courtesy, zealously seconded the efforts of the marchioness, and gave all his time as well as all his heart to the young children abandoned by their father.

Life was gentle and pleasant at Grosbois. The marchioness divided her time between the management of her fortune, which was placed in the hands of an old steward named Bonbonne, the most rigid observance of all the religious duties enjoined by austere piety, whose impulses were guided by an adroit spiritual director, Père Delar, a Camaldule monk, and the education of her two children, who promised to bear worthily a name made illustrious by great services rendered to the state.

Sometimes a letter, dashed off by the marquis in his hours of disgust, arrived to console his family, and to revive in the marchioness' heart an affection which she often reproached herself for not giving entirely to God.

Madame de Chauvelin still loved her husband, and when she had prayed all day Père Delar would call her attention to the fact that she had spoken to God of her beloved husband exclusively.

The marchioness had reached a point where she had ceased to expect or to hope for her husband on earth. She flattered herself, like the good, pious creature she was, that she deserved well enough of God to be permitted to join Monsieur de Chauvelin in the abode of everlasting joy.

The Camaldule looked sour at Monsieur Bonbonne and Monsieur Bonbonne at Abbé V——, when the children, being a little out of sorts or compelled to do penance, seemed to regret their father, although they knew him so little.

"It must be confessed," the monk would say to his penitent, "that that life will damn Monsieur de Chauvelin."

"It must be confessed," the old steward would say, "that the race he is running will ruin the family."

"Let us agree," the governor would say, "that these children will never attain glory, having never known what emulation is."

And the angelic marchioness would smile at all three, replying to the monk that Monsieur de Chauvelin would redeem himself in time; to the steward that the savings effected at Grosbois would relieve the faintness of the strong-box which had been bled so freely at Paris; to the tutor, that the children came of good stock, and that good blood is incapable of lying.

And during all this time the centenary oaks and the fragile nurslings were growing at Grosbois, alike deriving their sap and their life from the fruitful bosom of God.

An unhappy day arrived. On that day the flowers in the park, the fruit in the garden, the waters of the basin, and the very stones of the château withered and became bitter and gloomy. It was a day of confusion in the family. The steward Bonbonne presented accounts of a terrifying nature to the marchioness, and predicted ruin for her children if Monsieur de Chauvelin did not make haste to put his affairs in order.

"Madame," he said after breakfast, "allow me to say twenty words to you."

"Say on, my dear Bonbonne," the marchioness replied.

"Remember, madame," interposed Père Delar, "that I await you in the chapel."

"And I have the honor to remind Madame la

Marquise," said Abbé V——, "that we arranged for
an examination to-day in mathematics and grammar.
Otherwise these two young gentlemen will do no
work."

The two Messieurs de Chauvelin were beginning to
rebel against Latin and science on the pretext that their
father did not care whether they were learned men or
not.

The marchioness began by taking Père Delar's arm.

"Father," said she, "I will begin with you. My
confession will be a short one, thank God! Here it is:
Yesterday my mind wandered during divine service."

" Why so, my daughter ? "

"Because I expected a letter from Monsieur de
Chauvelin and it did not come."

" Be absolved, if that is all, my daughter."

" That is all," the marchioness replied with a seraphic
smile.

The monk withdrew.

" And now for you, Monsieur l'Abbé. The examination would be long and painful. The children, if they
complain, do not know their lessons. If they do not
know them, and you should prove it to me, I should be
compelled to scold them or punish them. Spare them
and ourselves. Let us postpone the test to some day
when it will be satisfactory to us all."

Monsieur l'abbé agreed that madame la marquise
was right. He disappeared like the monk, who was
already passing out of sight in the hazy depths of the
green arcades.

" Now it is your turn, Bonbonne," said the marchioness. " You are the only one left. Shall I settle
matters as easily with your forbidding expression and
your deep sighs ? "

"I doubt it."

"Ah! well, let us see?"

"It is a simple matter. My accounts are alarmingly true."

"Frighten me, if you can. You have never succeeded in frightening my private cash-box."

"Your cash-box will be frightened this month, madame. It will be more than frightened; it will die."

"Nonsense! have you taken me into the account too?" rejoined the marchioness, trying to jest.

"Have I taken you into the account? I should think so; that's a terrible obstacle!"

"I have never, never said a word to any one, Bonbonne."

"Better if you had! But I had no need for you to speak to know all about it."

"About what?"

"The amount of your savings."

"I defy you to tell me!" cried the marchioness blushing.

"If that is so, I will go straight to the point. You have about seventy-five thousand francs."

"O Bonbonne!" said the marchioness in a grieved tone, as if the steward had indiscreetly discovered a painful secret.

"Madame la Marquise does not suspect me, I trust, of having meddled with her papers."

"If not — how?"

"How much have you a year for your housekeeping? Is it not thirty thousand francs?"

"Yes."

"How much do you spend? Twenty-four thousand, do you not?"

" Yes."

" And you have been hoarding the difference for ten years, have you not, as Monsieur de Chauvelin has been ten years at court? "

" Yes."

" Very well, then, madame, with the compound interest you have, or should have, about seventy-five thousand francs."

" Bonbonne! "

" I have guessed right. Now, if you have them, you will give them to Monsieur de Chauvelin at his first request. And if you give them to him, there will be nothing left for your children in case the marquis should be suddenly stricken."

" Bonbonne! "

" Let us speak frankly! Your property is pledged. Monsieur de Chauvelin is pledged for seven hundred thousand francs."

" He possesses sixteen hundred thousand."

" Very good. But the excess over seven hundred thousand francs will not satisfy his creditors."

" You frighten me! "

" I am trying to."

" For what purpose? "

" So that you will beg Monsieur de Chauvelin, who spends too much, to put in trust at once for the benefit of your children, the remaining nine hundred thousand francs; to beg him to assign them to you as a jointure, or to leave them to you by will."

" By will? great heaven! "

" There you are with your scruples! Need a man die because he makes a will? "

" To think of mentioning a will to Monsieur de Chauvelin! "

"That's it! You are afraid of disturbing monsieur le marquis in his pleasure, in his digestion, in his favor at court, by those horrid words, *the future,* which always sound in happy moments like the word death. Ah! if you fear that, why, you will ruin your children; but you will have spared monsieur le marquis' ears."

"Bonbonne!"

"I am a talking column of figures. Listen to my accounts."

"It is horrible."

"It would be more horrible to wait for what I tell you is imminent. Play the part of a judicious adviser. Take your carriage and go to see monsieur le marquis."

"In Paris?"

"No, at Versailles."

"What! I, in the society my husband frequents? Never!"

"Write, then."

"Will he so much as read my letter? Alas! when I write to congratulate him or to tell him how I long for him, he does n't read what I write. What will he do when I take the pen as a man of business?"

"Let some friend do it then; myself, for instance."

"You?"

"Oh! do you mean to tell me that he won't listen to me? Oh! yes, madame, he will listen to me."

"You will make him ill, Bonbonne."

"His doctor will cure him."

"You will make him angry and anger will kill him."

"No, no! I am too anxious for him to live. If I kill him, it won't be until after I have made him write his will."

And the worthy man indulged in a loud laugh which wounded the marchioness.

"Bonbonne, if you speak so, I am the one you will kill," she murmured.

Bonbonne took her hand respectfully.

"Forgive me," he said. "I forgot myself, Madame la Marquise. Order the horses to be put to the carriage and I will start for Versailles."

"Ah! God be praised! You will take my books, and — but look!"

"What is it?"

"Can it be that my orders are anticipated?"

"How so?"

"You spoke of my carriage?"

"Yes."

"There it is in the Avenue du Mail."

"Ah!"

"The family livery."

"Those are monsieur le marquis' iron-gray horses."

"Madame, madame!" cried Abbé V——.

"Madame, madame!" cried Père Delar.

"Madame, madame!" cried twenty voices from the offices, the gardens, and the park.

"Mamma, mamma!" cried the children.

"Monsieur le marquis! oh, can it be true?" murmured the marchioness. "He at Grosbois to-day!"

"Good-morning, madame," said the marquis at a distance. His carriage had stopped, and he alighted joyously with eager gestures.

"It is himself, sound in body and cheerful in mind. I thank thee, O my God!"

"We thank thee, O God!" repeated the twenty voices which had announced the coming of the master and father.

VIII.

THE GAMBLER'S OATH.

IT was the marquis himself. He affectionately embraced his two children, who had uttered cries of joy when they saw him, and he bestowed upon the hand of the bewildered marchioness a kiss that came from his heart.

"You, monsieur! you," she said, taking possession of his arm.

"Myself! But the children were playing or studying. I do not wish to interrupt their studies, much less their play."

"Ah! monsieur, let us allow them to enjoy your dear presence to the full during the short time they have to see you."

"God be thanked, madame, they will see me for a long time."

"A long time — until to-morrow evening — do you mean it? You will not go until to-morrow evening?"

"Better than that, madame."

"You will sleep two nights at Grosbois?"

"Two nights, four nights, always."

"O monsieur, what can have happened?" cried the marchioness eagerly, not reflecting that such surprise on her part might be construed as a reproach for Monsieur de Chauvelin's past conduct.

The marquis frowned for a moment, then suddenly asked, with a smile, —

"Have you not prayed God to bring me back to my family?"

" O monsieur, always ! "

" Very well, madame, your prayers have been granted. It seemed to me that a voice was calling me and I obeyed that voice."

" And you have left the court ? "

" I have come to make my home at Grosbois," the marquis replied, choking back a sigh.

" What happiness for the dear children, for myself, for all the servants !   Ah ! monsieur, allow me to believe that it is true, let me enjoy that felicity."

" Your satisfaction, madame, is a balm that cures all my wounds.   But, tell me, are you willing to talk of household affairs a little ? "

"By all means, by all means," said the marchioness, pressing his hands.

" It seemed to me that I saw some very sorry-looking horses by the postern of the half-moon; are they yours ? "

" They are mine, monsieur."

" Horses too old for use ! "

" They are the horses you gave me when our son was born, monsieur."

" They were four and a half then; that was nine years ago, so the beasts are fourteen years old.   Fie ! such a team for you, marchioness ! "

" Ah, monsieur, when I go to mass, they succeed even now in running away."

" I saw three, I think."

" I gave the fourth, which is more spirited, to my son for his riding-lessons."

" My son learn to ride on a coach-horse !   Marchioness, marchioness, what sort of a horseman will you make of him ? "

The marchioness lowered her eyes.

"And do you no longer drive with four horses? You have eight, I think, and two saddle horses."

"True, monsieur; but as there are no hunting parties or riding parties during your absence, I reflected that by giving up four horses, two grooms, and a saddler, I could save six thousand francs a year."

"Six thousand francs, marchioness," murmured Monsieur de Chauvelin, ill-pleased.

"That is enough to board and lodge twelve families," she replied.

He took her hand.

"Always kind-hearted, always perfect! Whatever you do on earth is always inspired by God on high. But the Marquise de Chauvelin ought not to save money."

She raised her head.

"You mean to imply," he continued, "that I spend money freely. It is true, I do spend a great deal of money, and you are in want."

"I do not say that, monsieur."

"That must be the truth, marchioness. Noble and generous as you are, you would not have dismissed my servants unless from necessity. A groom discharged means one pauper more. You have been in want of money. I will talk with Bonbonne about it; but from this day forth you shall never be in that condition again. I will spend at Grosbois what I have spent at court, and instead of taking care of twelve families, you shall take care of two hundred."

"Monsieur —"

"And, I believe, thank God! that there will be grain enough left for twelve good horses which I own, and which will come to-morrow and live in your stables. Did you not say something about repairing the château?"

"The reception-rooms would need to be furnished anew."

"All my furniture from Paris will come this week. I will give dinner parties twice a week; we will hunt."

"You know, monsieur, that I am a little afraid of society," said the marchioness, alarmed at the idea of seeing all the uproarious friends from Versailles, whom she looked upon as her husband's capital sins.

"You shall name the guests yourself, marchioness. Now Bonbonne will give you the books; you will have the kindness to combine in one account the expenses at Paris and those at Grosbois."

The marchioness, wild with joy, tried to answer and could not. She took Monsieur de Chauvelin's hands, kissed them, probed the lowest depths of his soul with tear-dimmed eyes, and yielded to the blissful power of that warm atmosphere of pure love which penetrates everything it touches, and carries animation and a sense of well-being to the coldest extremities.

"Let us think of the children," he said; "how do you succeed in managing them?"

"Very well; the abbé is a bright man, his ideas are profound. Shall I present him to you?"

"Present all the household to me, yes, marchioness."

The marchioness waved her hand, and in a moment they saw the tutor approaching along the shady avenue where he had disappeared with the children; one of his hands rested on the shoulder of each child.

There was in the bearing and graceful motion of that young oak between the two reeds a something agreeably suggestive of the paternal relation, which pleased the marquis immensely.

"Monsieur l'abbé," said the marchioness, "let me tell

6

you some good news. Monsieur le Marquis here, our lord and master, proposes to remain with us."

"God be praised!" replied the abbé. "But alas! monsieur, can it be that the king is dead?"

"No, thank heaven! But I have bidden adieu to the court and the world. I remain here with my children. I am tired of living only in the mind and by ambition; I propose to try the heart for a while, so here I am among you. To begin with, monsieur l'abbé, are you satisfied with your pupils?"

"As well satisfied as it is possible to be, Monsieur le Marquis."

"So much the better. Make of them good Christians like their mother, upright men like their grandfather."

"And men of intellect, of merit, and of talent like their father," said the abbé. "I hope to accomplish all that."

"You are an invaluable man, then, abbé. And how are you, my old Bonbonne, — still a chronic grumbler? When I was no older than these boys you wanted to initiate me into the mysteries of business. I ought to have done as you wished, and then I should n't have been in such need of your experience to-day."

The children were dancing about on the grass with all the heedless gayety of their age. Their father followed their movements with an eye softened by emotion, and murmured, after a moment's silence, —

"Dear boys, I will never leave you again."

"May God grant that you speak the truth, Monsieur le Marquis!" said a grave, deep voice behind him.

Monsieur de Chauvelin turned and found himself facing a white-frocked monk, with a calm, stern face, who saluted him after the manner of monks.

"Who is this holy father?" the marquis asked his wife.

"Père Delar, my confessor."

"Ah! your confessor," he repeated, losing color some-what. Then, in a lower tone, he added, "I need a con-fessor myself, and monsieur is most welcome."

The monk, an adroit man, and accustomed to the ways of the great, knew better than to comment on the remark, but he registered it in his memory. Having been advised of the condition of affairs some days before by the steward, he determined to undertake the negotiation, and not to let slip so promising an opportunity of attending to God's business, the marchioness', and, it might be, his own as well.

"May I venture to ask you for news of the king, Monsieur le Marquis?" queried the monk.

"Why so, father?"

"Because there is a rumor that Louis XV. is likely soon to render an account of his reign to God. Such rumors are ordinarily the precursors of Providence. His Majesty has not long to live, believe me."

"Is that your belief, father?" said Monsieur de Chauvelin, more and more depressed.

"It is much to be desired, therefore, that he amend his scandalous ways, that he repent — "

"Monsieur," the marquis hastily interrupted, "confes-sors should wait in silence until they are summoned."

"Death does not wait, monsieur, and I have long been awaiting a word from you, but it does not come."

"Oh! my confession will be a long one, but it is not yet ripe."

"Confession consists entirely in repentance, in regret for having sinned; and the greatest of all sins, as I have told you, is behavior that causes scandal."

"Oh! as for scandal, everybody causes more or less. There is not one of us who does not furnish food for evil·

speaking. Heaven does not intend to punish us for the lying tongues of other people."

"Heaven punishes disobedience to its laws, heaven punishes impertinence. It sends us warnings; if we neglect them nothing can save us."

Monsieur de Chauvelin did not reply, but seemed lost in reflection. The marchioness, seeing that the conversation was fairly inaugurated, discreetly withdrew, praying God with all her heart that it might bear fruit. After a long minute's silence, during which the monk watched him closely, Monsieur de Chauvelin turned abruptly to him.

"Look you, father," he said, "I believe that you are right. I repent of having been young too long, and I mean to confess to you, for I feel, I feel that death is near at hand."

"Death! you believe that death is near, and you take no steps to ensure your soul's salvation, or to arrange for the disposition of your fortune. You fear death, and yet you do not think of making the will which is indispensable in the condition of affairs which you have created for your heirs. Pardon me, Monsieur le Marquis, my zeal and my devotion to your illustrious family carry me over far perhaps."

"No, you are right once more, father; but, have no fear, the will is made; I have only to sign it."

"You fear death, and you are not in a condition to appear before God."

"May he have mercy on me! I was born in the Christian religion and I wish to die a Christian. Come to-morrow, I beg you, and we will continue this interview, which will give rest to my soul."

"To-morrow? why to-morrow? Death does not pause or turn back."

"I need to collect my thoughts. I can not forget so quickly the life I have led; perhaps I long for it. Thanks for your counsel, father; it will bear fruit."

"God grant it! but you know the wise man's motto: Never postpone till to-morrow what can be done to-day."

"I already owe you a debt of gratitude. I was cast down, you have raised me; everything cannot be done at once, father."

"Ah! Monsieur le Marquis," replied the monk bowing, "but a moment is required to make of the culprit a penitent; of the damned, one of the elect; if you choose — "

"Very good, very good, father, to-morrow. There is the dinner-bell."

He dismissed him with a gesture and walked hastily into one of the paths. The tutor approached Père Delar.

"What is the matter with monsieur le marquis? I should not know him; he, who was always so animated, is anxious, depressed, and haggard."

"He has a presentiment that his end is near, and he is thinking about mending his ways. It will be a magnificent conversion, and will bring much honor to my convent. Oh! if the king — "

"Aha! the appetite seems to come with eating, father. I fear, however, that your longings will remain unsatisfied in that direction. His Majesty is a hard man to convince, and then, too, he has his own converters. Monseigneur the Bishop of Senez is spoken of as a hardy champion."

"Oh! the king is n't so incredulous as you claim. Do you remember his illness at Metz, and the dismissal of Madame de Châteauroux?"

"Yes, but Louis XV. was young then, and it was not a question of dislodging Jeanne Vaubernier, — two considerations which make an immense difference. How·

ever, you have time enough to think about it, dear Monsieur Delar; meanwhile, as dinner has been announced, we must not keep monsieur le marquis waiting. He does n't dine with us often, God knows! "

The father, mother, and children were assembled at the dinner table, where Père Delar and Abbé V—— arrived in good time. The marchioness had never seemed so happy; never had she exerted herself to such good effect to do the honors of her table.

The cook had surpassed himself. Fine fish from the artificial ponds, fat chickens from the poultry-yard, the most luscious fruits of hothouse and garden reminded the marquis what excellent cheer the house afforded when a cherished master was to be entertained.

The valets, proud of the illustrious service they were about to resume, strutted about in their newest liveries, and watched the master's eyes for the slightest sign of a wish to be anticipated, of an annoyance to be guarded against.

But the marquis soon lost the hearty appetite of which he had boasted after his arrival; the table seemed deserted to him; the respectful, happy silence seemed to him the silence of deathly dulness. Gradually his heart and his features alike were invaded by melancholy; he let his inert hand fall beside his still laden plate, and forgot the glasses in which the wines of Aï and of Burgundy, thirty years old, sparkled in diamonds and rubies.

From melancholy the marquis arrived at downright despondency; every one followed with alarm the painful progress of his depression.

A tear suddenly started from his eyes and wrung a sigh from the marchioness. He did not notice it.

"I have been reflecting," he suddenly said to his wife. "I want to be buried, not at Boissy-Saint-Léger with my father and mother, but in the Carmelite church on Place Maubert, Paris, with my ancestors."

"Why do you think about such things, monsieur? We have time enough for that, I imagine," said the marchioness, choked with grief.

"Who knows? Let some one call Bonbonne and tell him to wait for me in my large study. I propose to work with him for an hour. Père Delar pointed out to me the necessity of so doing. You have an excellent confessor in him, madame."

"I am happy that he meets your approval, monsieur; you can address yourself to him with perfect confidence."

"I will do so, and no later than to-morrow. With your permission, madame, I will go to my apartments."

The marchioness raised her eyes and thanked God in a mental prayer. She looked after her husband as he left the room with Bonbonne, and said, turning to her sons, —

"To-night, my children, ask God to inspire your father with the desire to remain permanently among us, to keep him in the same frame of mind in which he now is, and to give him grace to carry out his purposes."

"Come, my old Bonbonne," said the marquis when he was in his study, "to work, to work!"

He turned over all the papers with feverish eagerness, trying to identify and arrange them.

"There, there!" said the old man; "as we 're on the right road, my dear master, let us not go too fast; we lose time by going too fast, you know."

"Time presses, Bonbonne. I tell you, time presses."

"Nonsense."

"I tell you that the man to whom God grants the blessed joy of preparing for his last journey can never work quickly enough. Make haste, Bonbonne, let 's to work."

"At this rate, with this heat, monsieur, you will have pleurisy or congestion of the lungs or a sharp attack of fever, and in that way you will succeed in having your will made just in time."

"No more delay. Where is the account of receipts?"

"Here."

"And of outlay?"

"Here."

"Sixteen hundred thousand francs deficit? The devil!"

"Two years of economical living will fill the hole."

"I have n't two years to economize."

"Oh! you will drive me mad! What, with such health as yours?"

"Did n't you tell me that the notary had made a very ingenious draft of a will, in that it assured my sons the whole of the property at their majority?"

"Yes, monsieur, if you will give up for six years a fourth of the revenue from the real estate only."

"Let me see the draft."

"Here it is."

"My eyes are a little weak. Won't you read it to me yourself?"

Bonbonne began to read it article by article; the marquis from time to time expressed the liveliest satisfaction.

"The scheme is an excellent one," he said, at last, "especially as it gives Madame de Chauvelin three hundred thousand francs a year, twice what she now has."

"You approve it then?"

"In every respect."

"So that I can transcribe it?"

"Transcribe it."

"And then you must give it validity by putting your hand to it."

"Do it quickly, Bonbonne, do it quickly!"

"Why, you are absolutely unreasonable. It took me half an hour to read the document to you. I must have at least an hour to copy it."

"Oh! if you knew what haste I am in! Come, dictate to me, I will write it all with my own hand."

"By no means, monsieur, by no means, your eyes are red already; if you should write for quarter of an hour you would have a fever on the heels of the headache you are going to have."

"What shall I do during the hour that you think you require?"

"Go for a walk, take the air on the lawn with madame la marquise. I will cut my pens, and woe to the paper! I will blacken more of it, all by myself, I promise you, than three attorney's clerks."

The marquis followed the suggestion with a sort of repugnance; he felt dull and heavy, yet strangely agitated.

"Be calm, pray," said Bonbonne. "Are you afraid you won't have time to sign? An hour, I tell you. What the deuce! Monsieur le Marquis, surely you will live sixty-one minutes."

"You are right," he replied, and he went downstairs.

The marchioness was awaiting him. Seeing that he was calmer and his face brighter, she said,—

"Well, monsieur, have you been hard at work?"

"Oh! yes, marchioness, and at useful work, with which you and your sons will be content, I trust."

"So much the better! give me your arm. Shall we walk? The hothouses are open; would you like to pay them a visit?"

"Whatever you please, marchioness."

"You will sleep well after the walk. If you knew how delighted the servants were to put sheets on your great bed."

"I shall sleep as I have not slept for ten years, marchioness; I tremble with pleasure simply to think of it."

"You think that you will not be too much bored here with us?"

"No, marchioness, no."

"And that you will get used to our country ways?"

"Yes, without any difficulty. And if the king, whom I regret having treated somewhat rudely, perhaps,—if the king forgets me, he will do well."

"The king? Ah! monsieur," said the marchioness affectionately, "you sighed when you spoke of His Majesty."

"I love the king, marchioness, but believe me —"

He did not finish the sentence. The cracking of a whip and the sound of a horse's bells interrupted him.

"What is that?" he said.

"A courier just passing through the gate," the marchioness replied. "Is he in your service?"

"No; it is strange. A courier whom everybody salutes, who is allowed to enter the flower-garden, can come only from —"

"From the king!" murmured the marchioness, turning pale.

"In the king's name!" cried the courier in a loud voice.

"The king!"

Monsieur de Chauvelin hurried toward the courier, who had already handed his letter to the maître d'hôtel.

"A letter from the king, alas!" said the marchioness to Père Delar, whom the noise of the arrival had attracted with the rest.

The marquis offered the courier wine in a silver goblet, an honor explained by the respect accorded by every gentleman to royalty, even when represented by a servant.

He opened the letter; it contained these lines written in the monarch's own hand:—

"It is hardly twenty-four hours since you went away, my friend, and it seems as if I had not seen you for months. Old men who love each other ought not to part. Will they have time to join each other again? I am sad unto death. I need you; come, do not deprive me of a friend on the pretext of wishing to defend my crown. It is the surest way to attack it, on the contrary, and, so long as you sustain it by your presence, I shall feel that it is firmer than ever. Let me see you to-morrow at my *lever;* that will be a sign of a happy day.

"Your most affectionate

"Louis."

"The king summons me," said Chauvelin, deeply moved. "I must go instantly; he cannot do without me. Let my horses be harnessed!"

"Oh!" rejoined the marchioness, "so soon, after so many sweet promises!"

"You shall hear from me soon, madame."

"Monsieur le Marquis, the copy is made!" cried Bonbonne in the distance.

"Very well! very well!"

"You have only to read it over and sign it."

"I have n't the time. Later."

"Later! Why remember what you said just now."

"I know it, I know it."

"'No more delay.'"

"The king cannot wait."

"But you forget your children, you forget the fate of your family."

"I forget nothing, Bonbonne; but I must go, and I am going. My children and the future of my family are all cared for, Bonbonne, remember that."

"A signature, only a signature."

"You see, my old friend," said the marquis, radiant with joy, "I am so determined to arrange that matter, that if I should die before I have signed my will, I swear to you that I will return from the other world, and that is far away, for the express purpose of signing it. Let that set your mind at rest; adieu."

Hastily embracing his children and his wife, forgetting everything except king and court, he jumped into his carriage as if he had grown twenty years younger, and started for Paris.

The marchioness and the whole household, but now so joyous and happy, remained by the gate, deserted, depressed, dumb with despair.

IX.

VENUS AND PSYCHE.

ON the morning following the despatch of his letter to Grosbois, the first words spoken by Louis XV. were an inquiry for the Marquis de Chauvelin, and his first glance was in search of him.

The marquis had arrived during the night and was present at the *petit lever.*

"Good," said the king, "there you are, marquis. *Mon Dieu!* what a long time you have been away!"

"It is my first absence, sire, and shall be my last; if I leave you now it will be forever. But the king is very kind to think that I have been long absent. I have been away only twenty-four hours."

"Do you mean it, dear friend? In that case it must be that devilish prediction ringing in my ears; so that, failing to see you at your usual post, I imagined that you were dead, and, with you dead, — you understand?"

"Perfectly, sire."

"Let us say no more about that. You are here and that's the main thing. To be sure the countess has a little grudge against us: against you for saying what you said, against me for recalling you after such an insult; but don't you worry over her ill-humor, for time arranges all those things and the king will assist time."

"Thanks, sire."

"Tell me what you did during your exile."

"Fancy, sire, that I came near being converted!"

"I understand: you are beginning to repent of having sung of the seven mortal sins."

"Oh! if I had never done aught but sing of them!"

"My cousin Conti was talking about the song only yesterday, and he was delighted with it."

"I was young then, sire, and impromptus seemed easy to me. I was alone at Ile-Adam with seven charming women. Monsieur le Prince de Conti hunted, while I remained at the château and — wrote poetry. Ah! those were the good old days, sire."

"Do you take me for your confessor, marquis, and is this your confession?"

"My confessor? Ah! yes, Your Majesty is right, I had made an appointment for this morning with a Camaldule at Grosbois."

"Oh, the poor man! what an opportunity to learn something he has missed! Would you have told him everything, Chauvelin?"

"Absolutely everything, sire."

"It would have been a long session in that case."

"Oh, *mon Dieu!* sire, in addition to my own sins, I have so many sins of other people on my conscience, especially so many of —"

"Of mine, eh? I excuse you from confessing those, Chauvelin; a man confesses for himself only."

"Nevertheless, sire, sin is alarmingly epidemic at court. I no sooner arrive than I hear of a very strange adventure."

"An adventure, Chauvelin; to whose account is it charged?"

"To whose account are interesting adventures usually charged, sire?"

"*Parbleu!* to mine, I suppose."

"Or to the —"

"Or to the Comtesse du Barry's, eh ? "

"You have guessed, sire."

"What do you say? the Comtesse du Barry has sinned ? *Peste!* tell me about it, Chauvelin."

" I don't say that the adventure was exactly a sin in itself, I say that it came to my mind apropos of sinning."

"Well, what is the adventure, marquis? tell me at once."

" At once, sire ? "

" Yes. Kings, as you know, do not like to wait."

" *Peste !* it is a serious matter, sire."

" Bah ! has she had some new dispute with my grand-daughter-in-law ? "

" Sire, I do not say no."

" Ah ! the countess will end by falling out with the dauphiness, and then, on my word ! — "

" I think, sire, that madame la comtesse has already had a falling out."

" With the dauphiness ? "

" No, but with another of your granddaughters-in-law."

" The Comtesse de Provence ? "

" Herself."

" The devil! I am in a pretty pickle, then! Tell me, Chauvelin — "

" Sire ? "

" Is the Comtesse de Provence the complainant ? "

" They say so."

" Then the Comte de Provence is sure to write some outrageous verses on the poor countess. She has only to keep still, she will be lashed in fine style."

" That will be simply a Roland for an Oliver, sire."

" I beg your pardon ? "

" Imagine that Madame la Marquise de Rosen — "

"The fascinating little brunette, the Comtesse de Provence's friend?"

"Yes, whom Your Majesty has had your eyes on much of the time during the past month."

"Oh! I have been scolded sufficiently for that in a certain place, marquis! Well?"

"Who has scolded you, sire?"

"*Pardieu!* the countess."

"Very good. The countess has scolded you, sire, — so far so good; but in the other direction she has done something more than scold."

"Explain yourself, marquis; you frighten me."

"*Dame!* sire, you may well be frightened; I don't say you nay."

"Is it really serious?"

"Very serious."

"Speak."

"It seems that —"

"That?"

"You see, sire, it is harder to tell about than it was to do."

"You really do alarm me, marquis. Thus far I have thought that you were joking. But if something really serious has happened let us talk seriously."

At that moment the Duc de Richelieu entered the room.

"Something new, sire!" he said, with a smile that was at once winning and anxious: winning because he wished to propitiate the king, anxious because he was about to contest the favor of this favorite who had been recalled to Versailles after a single day of banishment.

"Something new! where does it come from, my dear duke?" said the king.

He looked around and saw the Marquis de Chauvelin laughing in his sleeve.

"You laugh, heartless man," he said.

"Sire, the storm is about to burst; I foresee that from the melancholy air of Monsieur de Richelieu."

"You are mistaken, marquis. I announced news, it is true, but I do not undertake to tell what it is."

"However am I to know what you are talking about then?"

"A page from Madame de Provence is in your antechamber with a letter from his mistress; what are Your Majesty's orders?"

"Oho!" said the king, who was not sorry to throw the whole burden upon Monsieur or Madame de Provence, whom he did not like, "since when have the sons of France or their wives been accustomed to write to the king instead of presenting themselves at his *lever?*"

"Sire, the letter will probably explain to Your Majesty that failure to observe the rules of etiquette."

"Take the letter, duke, and hand it to me."

The duke bowed, left the room, and returned a moment later with the letter in his hand.

"Sire," he said, handing the letter to the king, "do not forget that I am Madame du Barry's friend, and that I constitute myself her advocate in advance."

The king glanced at Richelieu, opened the letter, and frowned visibly as he ran his eye over its contents.

"Oh! this is too much," he muttered; "and you have undertaken to defend a bad cause, duke. In very truth, Madame du Barry is mad."

He turned to the officers of his household.

"Let some one go at once to Madame de Rosen's and inquire for her health in my name, and say to her that I will receive her immediately after I am dressed, before going to mass. Poor marchioness! dear little woman!"

7

The bystanders exchanged glances. Was a new star rising above the horizon of royal favor?

In truth, nothing was more likely. The marchioness was young and pretty. She had been appointed lady-in-waiting to Madame de Provence a year before, and had become intimate with the favorite, attending all her private functions, where the king had seen her frequently. But, upon certain observations on the part of the princess, who was offended by that intimacy, she suddenly broke off all relations with Madame du Barry, who had made no secret of her annoyance.

That is all that the court knew.

The letter, of which nobody knew the contents, made a serious impression on the king. He seemed thoughtful during the remainder of the reception, spoke a word or two only to some of his particular favorites, hurried the ceremonial, and dismissed those in attendance earlier than usual, after bidding Monsieur de Chauvelin not to go away.

The ceremony of the *lever* at an end, everybody departed, and as His Majesty was informed that Madame de Rosen was waiting, he gave orders to introduce her.

Madame de Rosen's *entrée* was as pathetic as possible; she was weeping bitterly as she knelt at the king's feet.

The king raised her.

"Forgive me, sire," she said, "for having made use of an august influence to obtain access to Your Majesty; but really I was so desperate — "

"Oh! I forgive you with all my heart, madame, and I am obliged to my grandson for opening a door for you, which will always be open to you henceforth. But let us come down to the fact, — to the main point."

The marchioness cast down her eyes.

"I am in haste," continued the king; "my presence

is awaited at mass. Is what you write to me really true? Can it be that the countess really permitted herself to — "

" O sire, you make me blush with shame. I come to demand justice at the king's hands. Never was a woman of quality so treated."

" What! " said the king, smiling in spite of himself, " treated like a disobedient child, and spared no detail? "

" Yes, sire, by four of her women in her presence, in her boudoir," replied the young woman, lowering her eyes.

" Peste ! " rejoined the king, in whose mind that last detail gave birth to a multitude of ideas, " the countess did not boast of that project beforehand. And how was it done? tell me, marchioness, " he added, with the leer of a satyr.

" Sire, " replied the young woman, blushing more and more, " she asked me to breakfast. I excused myself on the ground that I had little liberty, that my duties required me to be in attendance on Her Royal Highness at eight o'clock in the morning. She sent word to me to come at seven, that she would not detain me long; and, in fact, sire, I stayed with her only half an hour."

" You can set your mind at rest, madame, I will have an explanation with the countess, and justice shall be done you. But I urge you, in your own interest, not to make too much noise over the incident; above all things, let your husband know nothing of it. Husbands are devilish prudes in such matters."

" Oh ! I beg the king to believe that, so far as I am concerned, I shall know enough to say nothing. But my enemy, the countess, — I am very sure that she has already boasted to her intimate friends of what she has done, and to-morrow the whole court will know. O my God ! my God ! how wretched I am ! "

And the marchioness hid her face in her hands at the risk of making her rouge spread with her tears.

"Have no fear, marchioness," said the king. "The court could have no prettier plaything than you. And if people do talk about it, it will be from envy, just as in Olympus long ago they talked about a similar adventure that happened to Psyche. I know some of our prudes who would not be so easily consoled as you can afford to be; for you had nothing to lose by it, marchioness."

The marchioness made a reverence and blushed still more, if such a thing were possible.

The king watched the blush and devoured the tears.

"Come," said he, "return to your apartments and wipe those pretty eyes. This evening, at the card-table, we will arrange it all; you have my promise to that effect."

And with the gallantry and winning manner peculiar to his race, the king escorted the young woman to the door, where she had to pass through the throng of courtiers, all of whom were surprised and puzzled to the last degree.

The Duc d'Ayen, who was captain of the body-guard in attendance, approached the king and bowed low without speaking, awaiting his orders.

"To mass, Duc d'Ayen, to mass, now that I have performed the functions of confessor," said the king.

"Such a pretty penitent can have committed none but pretty little sins, sire."

"Alas! the poor child! they are not her own sins that she is expiating," pursued the king, walking along the broad gallery toward the chapel.

The Duc d'Ayen followed a step behind him, near enough to hear and answer him, but not on the same line, as etiquette demanded.

"A man would be lucky to be her accomplice even in a crime, sire."

"Her sin is the countess'."

"Oho! the king knows all of those."

"The dear countess is certainly slandered. She is extravagant, mad if you will, — as on the occasion in question, for which I shall give her a scolding, — but she has an excellent heart. It would be useless for any one to tell me any ill of her, for I would not believe it. *Parbleu!* I know perfectly well that I am not her first lover, and that I succeeded Radix de Sainte-Foy in her good graces."

"Yes, sire," replied the duke, with his usual malice enveloped in the most exquisite courtesy, "as Your Majesty succeeded Pharamond."

The king, notwithstanding his shrewd wit, was not strong enough to contend with that rough jouster unless he lost his temper. He realized the absurdity of the latter course, and pretended not to understand. He made haste to address a word or two to a knight of Saint-Louis whom he passed. Louis XV. was good-humored and easy-going; he overlooked many liberties on the part of his intimate friends, and, provided that he was entertained, he cared little for the rest. The Duc d'Ayen especially possessed the privilege of saying whatever his fancy prompted him to say. Madame du Barry the omnipotent had never dreamed of opposing him; his name, his rank, and his wit seemed to her from the outset to make him unassailable.

During the mass the king's mind wandered. He thought of the tempest Madame du Barry's latest freak would arouse if it should come to the ears of monsieur le dauphin. That prince had administered a just rebuke only the day before to the countess, who had insisted that Vicomte du Barry should have an appointment as equerry in his (the dauphin's) household, against his will.

"Do not let him come near me," the dauphin had said, "or I will have him driven away by my people."

Certainly such a frame of mind gave little promise of indulgence for such a vulgar practical joke as that in which the countess had indulged. Louis XV. left the chapel, therefore, sorely perplexed. Before going to the council, he betook himself to the apartments of madame la dauphine. He found her gorgeously attired, with a bird's beak in diamonds, beautifully mounted, in her hair.

"You have a marvellous jewel there, madame," said the king.

"Do you think so, sire? How does it happen that Your Majesty does not recognize it?"

"I?"

"To be sure, since Your Majesty ordered it to be brought to me."

"I have no idea what you mean."

"I can very easily explain my meaning. Yesterday, a jeweller appeared at the château of Versailles with this jewel, adorned with fleurs-de-lis and the crown of France, which Your Majesty had ordered. Since God has taken away the queen, I alone, he thought, was entitled to wear it. He brought it to me, therefore, in accordance with your commands and your intention, I doubt not."

The king blushed and did not reply.

"Here is another evil omen," he thought. "The countess was well advised to provide fresh embarrassment for me with her absurd treatment of the marchioness. — Shall you come to the card-party this evening, madame?" he said aloud.

"If Your Majesty bids me do so."

"Bid you, my child! I beg you to come; you will give me great pleasure."

Madame la dauphine bowed coldly. The king saw that he could not succeed in making her unbend. He spoke of having to attend the council and took his leave.

"My children do not love me," he said to the Duc d'Ayen, who had not left him.

"The king is in error. I can assure Your Majesty that your august children love you at least as dearly as you love them."

Louis understood the epigram, but did not show that he understood it. That was the policy he had adopted. Otherwise, he would have had to banish the Duc d'Ayen ten times a day, and the king, after the ennui caused by Monsieur de Chauvelin's absence, understood better than ever how indispensable the presence of his favorite courtiers was to him.

"Bah!" he said to himself, "they can prick me all they like, they won't flay me. The thing will last as long as I do, and my successor may get out of it as best he can."

Strange recklessness, for which the ill-fated Louis XVI. was to pay a heavy penalty!

X.

THE KING'S CARD-PARTY.

WHEN he entered the countess' apartments, intending to scold her, the king was welcomed by an ill-humored countenance behind which he felt that a storm of anger was grumbling, all ready to break out.

Louis XV. was weak. He dreaded scenes, whether they came from his daughters, his grandsons, his daughters-in-law, or his mistress, and yet, like all men placed between their mistresses and their families, he constantly exposed himself to them.

On that day he proposed to anticipate the struggle that was preparing by providing himself with an auxiliary.

And so, after he had cast upon the countess the single glance by which he consulted the barometer of her good-humor he looked all about the room.

"Where is Chauvelin?" he asked.

"Monsieur de Chauvelin, sire?" said the countess.

"Yes, Monsieur de Chauvelin."

"Why, it seems to me, and you know it better than any one, that I am not the one to whom you should apply for news of Monsieur de Chauvelin, sire."

"Why so?"

"Why, because he is not one of my friends; and, he not being one of my friends, it follows naturally that you should look for him elsewhere than in my apartments."

" I told him to come and wait for me here."

" Oh, well! he must have taken the liberty to disobey the king's commands, and on my word! it was quite as well for him to disobey you as to come here to insult me, as he did the last time."

" Never mind, never mind; I want you to be reconciled," said the king.

" To Monsieur de Chauvelin? " asked the countess.

" To everybody, *morbleu !* "

Then, turning to the countess' sister, who was pretending to amuse herself setting porcelain figures in a line on a console, —

" Chon," he said.

" Sire."

" Come here, my child."

Chon drew near the king.

" Do me the favor, little sister, to send some one to fetch Monsieur de Chauvelin at once."

Chon bowed and left the room to carry out the king's wishes.

Madame du Barry tossed her head and turned her back on His Majesty.

" Well! what is there in that to vex you, countess? " queried the king.

" Oh! I understand," she replied, " that Monsieur de Chauvelin enjoys all your favor, and that you could not get along without him. He is so desirous to please you and so respectful to those you love! "

Louis felt that the storm was approaching. He tried to cut off the water-burst with a cannon shot.

" Chauvelin," he said, " is not the only one who fails in the respect due to me and to those who belong to me."

" Oh! I know," cried Madame du Barry. " Your

Parisians, your Parliament, your very courtiers, to say nothing of persons whom I do not choose to name, fail in respect to the king at their good pleasure, and vie with each other in showing their lack of respect."

The king glanced at the impertinent young woman with a feeling not wholly exempt from pity.

"Do you know, countess," he said, "that I am not immortal, and that you are playing a game that will lead to your being put in the Bastille or driven from the kingdom as soon as I have closed my eyes?"

"Bah!" exclaimed the countess.

"Oh, don't laugh, countess, it is as I tell you."

"Really, sire, how so?"

"I will state the case in two words."

"I await your statement, sire."

"What is this story of the Marquise de Rosen, and what sort of a liberty, in the most execrable taste, did you take with the poor woman? Do you forget that she has the honor to belong to the household of Madame la Comtesse de Provence?"

"Forget it, sire! No, indeed."

"Very well! then answer me. What is this naughty girl's punishment that you allowed yourself to inflict on the Marquise de Rosen?"

"I, sire?"

"Yes, you," said the king testily.

"Well, upon my word!" cried the countess. "I did not expect to be blamed for carrying out Your Majesty's orders."

"My orders!"

"Certainly. Does the king deign to remember what reply he made when I complained to him of the marchioness' discourtesy?"

"Faith! no. I have no idea."

"Very well! the king said to me: 'What can you expect, countess? The marchioness is a child who ought to be whipped.'"

"*Morbleu!* that was no reason for doing it," cried the king, blushing in spite of himself, for he remembered that he had said, word for word, what the countess had just repeated.

"Very good!" said the countess. "Your Majesty's slightest desire being equivalent to an order in the eyes of his most devoted servant, she made haste to execute that one like the others."

The king could not refrain from laughing at the countess' imperturbable gravity.

"So I am the culprit?" he asked.

"To be sure, sire."

"Then it is for me to expiate the offence."

"Apparently."

"So be it. In that case, countess, you will invite the marchioness to supper in my name, and you will place under her napkin the colonel's commission which her husband has been soliciting for six months, and which I certainly should not have given him so soon except for this incident. In that way reparation will be made for the insult."

"That is all very well! That takes care of the marchioness' insult, but how about mine?"

"What, yours?"

"Yes, who will make reparation for that?"

"How have you been insulted, I pray to know?"

"Oh, this is charming! pray feign surprise."

"I am not feigning it, my dear love. I am, in all frankness and seriousness, very much surprised."

"You have just come from madame la dauphine, have you not?"

"Yes."

"Then you know very well the trick she has played me."

"No, upon my honor! tell me."

"Well, yesterday my jeweller brought her a necklace and me a bird's beak of diamonds at the same time."

"What then?"

"What then?"

"Yes."

"What then, eh? Why, after taking her necklace, she asked to see my beak."

"Aha!"

"And as it had fleurs-de-lis for ornaments, she said, —

"'You are mistaken, my dear Monsieur Bœhmer; that beak of diamonds is not for the countess, but for me, and the proof of what I say is that it has the three fleurs-de-lis of France, which, since the queen's death, I alone have the right to wear.'"

"So that — "

"So that the jeweller, being frightened, dared not disobey the order of madame la dauphine to leave the diamond beak with her, and hurried hither to inform me that my diadem had caught on the way."

"Well! what do you expect me to do, countess?"

"Do! why, I want you to make her give me back my beak."

"Make her give you back your beak?"

"Certainly."

"The dauphiness? You are mad, my dear."

"What! I am mad?"

"Yes. I will give you another first."

"Oh! pshaw! I know what that means."

" On my honor as a gentleman ! I promise you."

" Yes! and I shall have it in a year, or in six months at the earliest. How amusing it is ! "

" Madame, let this delay be your warning."

" Warning of what ? "

" To be less ambitious in the future."

" I, ambitious ? "

" To be sure. You know what Monsieur de Chauvelin said the other day."

" Bah ! your Chauvelin talks nothing but nonsense."

" But, after all, who authorized you to wear the arms of France ? "

" What 's that ? who authorized me ? why, you."

" I ? "

" Yes, you ! The monkey you gave me the other day wore them on his collar; why should n't I wear them on my head ? Oh ! but I know where it all comes from ; somebody told me."

" What did somebody tell you ? Let us hear."

" *Parbleu!* your plans."

" Well, countess, tell me what my plans are. On my word of honor, it would please me greatly to know them."

" Will you deny that there is a scheme to marry you to the Princesse de Lamballe, and that Monsieur de Chauvelin and all the dauphin's and dauphiness' clique are trying to drive you to it ? "

" Madame," replied the king sternly, " I will not deny that there is some truth in what you say, and I will add that I might do much worse. You know it better than I, countess, for you have sounded me about another marriage."

That remark closed the countess' mouth. She sat

down, in ill-humor, at the other end of the room, and
broke two porcelain figures.

"Ah! Chauvelin was right," murmured the king.
"The crown is not well placed in the hands of
Cupids."

There was a moment of sulky silence, during which
Mademoiselle du Barry returned to the room.

"Sire," said she, "Monsieur de Chauvelin cannot be
found anywhere. I was told that he was in his own
apartments, but I have rung and called at his door to
no purpose. He refuses to reply."

"*O mon Dieu!*" cried the king. "Has any accident
happened to him? Is he ill? Go quickly, quickly,
and order the door broken in!"

"Oh! no, sire, he is not ill," replied the countess
sharply; "for, on leaving the Prince de Soubise and my
brother Jean in the Œil-de-Bœuf, he announced that
he should be at work all day on urgent business, but
that he would not fail to be at Your Majesty's card-
party this evening."

The king took advantage of what seemed to be a
proffered armistice on the countess' part.

"He is writing his confession, perhaps," he said,
"for the edification of his Camaldule. By the way,
countess," he added, "do you know that Bordeu's
medicine is doing marvels? Do you know that I do
not propose to use any other? A fig for Bonnard and
Lamartinière and all their dieting! The other will
make me young again, on my word!"

"Nonsense! sire," said Chon. "Why need Your
Majesty talk constantly of old age? *Mon Dieu!* is n't
Your Majesty of the same age as everybody else?"

"Well, well!" cried the king. "You are like that
great rascal of a D'Aumont, to whom I was complaining

the other day that I had no teeth: 'Why, sire,' he
replied, showing me a jaw like a porter's, 'who does
have teeth?'"

"I have," said the countess; "and I warn you that
I will bite you till the blood comes, if you continue to
sacrifice me to everybody in this way."

And she returned and seated herself beside the king,
displaying a row of pearls in which it was impossible
to see a threat.

And so the king, defying their bite, put his lips to
the countess' lovely red lips, just as she made a signal
to Chon. Chon picked up the pieces of the two
porcelain figures.

"There!" she said. "All that falls to the ground is
for him who picks it up. Really I think that Bordeu
must be a great man," she added under her breath,
as she cast a last glance at the king and countess.

And she went out, leaving her sister well advanced
on the path of reconciliation.

The king's card-party began at six o'clock in the
evening. Monsieur de Chauvelin kept his promise,
and was among the first to arrive. The countess
appeared in full court dress, because of the presence of
the dauphiness, who she knew was to be there.

The marquis and the countess met and greeted each
other in the most friendly way.

"*Mon Dieu!* Monsieur de Chauvelin," said the
countess, with one of those two-edged smiles which
courtiers sharpen so skilfully. "How red you are!
One would say you were on the verge of an attack of
apoplexy. See Bordeu, marquis. There's no hope for
you except in Bordeu."

She turned to the king with a smile that would have
led a pope to perdition.

"Ask the king," she said.

Monsieur de Chauvelin bowed.

"I certainly shall not fail to do so, madame."

"And in so doing you will fulfil the duty of a faithful subject. You must look to your health, my dear marquis, as you are to precede by only two months — "

"I wish that I were to be the one to go before you," said the king, "for then you would be sure to live a hundred years, Chauvelin. But I can only repeat the countess' advice: consult Bordeu, my friend, consult Bordeu."

"Sire, whatever the hour assigned for my death, — and God alone knows when any man is to die, — I promise the king that I will die at his feet."

"Fie, fie! Chauvelin, there are promises that are easily made but cannot be kept. Ask these ladies if it is not so; but if you are as melancholy as all that, my dear friend, we shall die of grief simply from looking at you. Come, Chauvelin, shall we play this evening?"

"As Your Majesty pleases."

"Would you like to whip me at a game of hombre?"

"At the king's service."

They went to the tables.

Monsieur de Chauvelin and the king took their places opposite each other at a special table.

"Now, Chauvelin, keep your eyes open," said the king. "Be ready for the parry. You may be ill, but I was never so well myself. I propose to be wildly gay. Look well to your money above all things. I have to pay Rotiers for a mirror and Bœhmer for a diamond beak."

Madame du Barry bit her lips.

But the marquis, instead of replying, rose painfully from his chair.

"It is very hot, sire," he muttered.

"True," replied the king, who, instead of losing his temper as Louis XIV. would have done at this infraction of the laws of etiquette, treated the difficulty from a selfish point of view. "It is very warm, Chauvelin, but I thank God for it, for the evenings are cool in the month of April."

The marquis tried to smile and picked up his cards with an effort.

"Come, Chauvelin," continued the king. "You are *hombre*."

"Yes, sire," faltered the marquis; and he bowed.

"Have you a good hand? Let us see. Ah! *ventre Saint-gris*, as my ancestor Henri IV. used to say, how disagreeable you are to-night!"

He glanced at his cards.

"Ah! my dear friend," he said, "I fancy that you are whipped this time."

The marquis made a violent effort to speak, and became so red that the king stopped in dismay.

"Why, what's the matter, Chauvelin?" he asked. "Answer me."

Monsieur de Chauvelin held out his hands, dropped his cards, drew a long breath, and fell face downward on the floor.

"Great heaven!" exclaimed the king.

"Apoplexy!" murmured certain officious courtiers.

They lifted the marquis, but he did not move a muscle.

"Take *that* away! take it away!" said the king in terror. "Take it away!"

He left the table, trembling nervously, and seized the

8

arm of the Comtesse du Barry, who led him away to her apartments, nor did he once turn his head to look at that friend from whom, only the night before, he could not bear to be separated.

The king having left the room, no one gave a thought to the lifeless marquis.

His body lay for some time hanging over the back of an arm-chair, for they had raised him to see if he were dead, and then had let him fall back.

The body produced a singular effect, alone in that deserted salon, amid the candelabra gleaming with light and flowers, filling the air with perfume.

A moment later a man appeared in the doorway of the salon, looked all around the room, saw the marquis lying on the chair, approached him, placed his hand on his heart, and said in a cold, clear voice, just as the great clock struck seven, —

"He has gone. A fine death, *cordieu!* a fine death!"

That man was the physician Lamartinière.

XI.

THE VISION.

On the morning of that same day Père Delar had arrived early at Grosbois, with the intention of saying mass at the chapel, and of leaving the praiseworthy disposition the marquis had shown the night before no time to cool. But Madame de Chauvelin met him and told him, with tears in her eyes, all her apprehensions concerning the salvation, already so endangered, of the neophyte who had escaped from their hands at the first friendly word sent to him by the king.

She kept her confessor to dinner, in order to talk with him more at length, and to derive from his wise advice the courage she so much needed after this last disappointment.

Madame de Chauvelin and Père Delar, after leaving the table, walked together in the park for a considerable time, and had seats carried to the shore of a lovely pond, in order to breathe the cool spring breeze after a warm day.

"Reverend father," said the marchioness, "notwithstanding all the comforting words you have said to me, Monsieur de Chauvelin's departure causes me much anxiety. I know how attached he is to life at court. I know that the king is all-powerful, not only over his mind, but over his heart, and His Majesty's conduct is so far from orderliness! I do not think it is a sin to speak so, father. Alas! the scandal is only too public!"

"I assure you, madame, that monsieur le marquis received a salutary impression. It was the first touch. Time and Providence will do the rest. I was speaking of him this morning to our reverend prior. He has ordered prayers in the convent. Do you pray, too, my daughter, you, who are most deeply interested in the great work. Let your children pray. Let us all pray. I offered the blessed sacrifice of the mass in the chapel of the château to that end, and I will do the same every day."

"In the twenty years that I have been Monsieur de Chauvelin's wife," rejoined the marchioness, "I have not let an hour pass without asking God to touch his heart. Thus far the Lord has not granted my prayers. I have lived alone, generally in sorrow and tears, as you know, father. I have lamented in solitude errors which I could not combat. God did not, it seems, deem me sufficiently pure to give me the victory. I must needs suffer still more to purchase that blessing. I will suffer! May the will of the Almighty be done!"

Meanwhile the children and their tutor were at some little distance from the marchioness and Père Delar, the tutor being little older than his charges, — he was only eighteen, — and sharing their amusements.

"Brother," said the elder, "do you know what the fashionable game is now at court?"

"Yes, of course I do. Father told me last night at supper; it is hombre."

"Well, let's play hombre."

"We can't. In the first place, we have to have cards, and in the second place, we don't know how to play."

"One player is *hombre*."

"And the other?"

"*Dame!* the other is afraid, I suppose, and then he loses."[1]

"Let's not talk about cards, brother. You know our mother doesn't like it, and she says cards bring bad luck."

At that moment Madame de Chauvelin rose.

"Mother is going into the park," said the younger boy, looking after her, "so she won't see us. Besides, monsieur l'abbé is right with us, and he would tell us if it were wrong."

"It is always wrong," said the tutor, "to give pain to one's mother."

"Oh! but my father plays at court," rejoined the child, with the persistent logic which clings like all weaknesses to every support that affords a little consolation. "We can play as long as my father plays."

The abbé had no reply at hand, and the child continued, —

"Look, there is mother just bidding Père Delar good-night. She's going toward the gate with him. He must be going home. Let's wait. When Père Delar has gone mamma will go to her oratory. We can go back to the château behind her, and we'll ask for some cards and play."

The children followed their mother with their eyes among the deepening shadows, where she gradually passed out of sight.

It was one of those charming evenings that precede the hot days of May. The trees, still leafless, gave promise of foliage near at hand in their swelling buds. Some, like the chestnuts and lindens, more

[1] There is no difference in pronunciation between *hombre* and *ombre*, which means *ghost*.

hurried than the rest, were beginning to burst their envelopes and put forth the springtime treasures they enclosed.

The air was calm and was beginning to be peopled with the ephemeral creatures that appear with the spring and disappear with the autumn. They could be seen disporting themselves by thousands in the last rays of the setting sun, which made of the river a broad purple and gold ribbon, while in the east, that is to say, toward that portion of the park where Madame de Chauvelin had passed out of sight, all objects were beginning to lose their distinctive outlines in that lovely bluish tint which belongs only to certain privileged periods of the year.

There was profound tranquillity blended with infinite splendor throughout all nature.

The silence was broken by the château clock striking seven, and the strokes vibrated a long while in the evening breeze.

Suddenly the marchioness, who was bidding the Camaldule good-night, uttered a loud cry.

"What is it?" inquired the reverend father, retracing his steps. "What is the matter, Madame la Marquise?"

"Nothing, nothing. O my God!"

And the marchioness visibly lost color.

"But you cried out. You certainly felt some shock, some sharp pain. Why, at this moment you are growing paler and paler. What is the matter? In heaven's name, what is the matter?"

"It is impossible. My eyes deceive me."

"What do you see? Tell me, tell me, madame."

"No, it is nothing."

The Camaldule persisted.

" Nothing nothing, I tell you," Madame de Chauvelin repeated, " nothing."

But her voice died away on her lips, and her eyes were fixed on vacancy, while her hand, white as a hand of ivory, rose slowly to point out an object which the monk could not see.

" In God's name," insisted Père Delar, " tell me what you see."

" Oh! I do not see anything. No, no; it is madness!" cried Madame de Chauvelin; " and yet — oh! look, pray look!"

" Where?"

" There, there, do you see?"

" I see nothing."

" You see nothing — there, there?"

" Absolutely nothing; but tell me, madame, what do you see?"

" Oh! I see — but no, it is impossible."

" Tell me."

" I see Monsieur de Chauvelin in court dress, but very pale and walking very slowly. He passed along there, over there."

" My God!"

" Without seeing me, do you understand? Or, even if he saw me, without speaking to me, which is stranger still."

" And do you see him now?"

" Yes."

And the marchioness' finger and her eyes indicated the direction followed by the marquis, who was still invisible to Père Delar.

" Where is he going, madame?"

" Toward the château. He is just passing the great oak yonder. He brushes against the bench. Look,

look, he is going toward the children. He turns away behind the clump of trees. He has disappeared. Oh! if the children are still where they were, it was impossible for them not to see him."

At that instant a loud cry made Madame de Chauvelin start. The cry was uttered by the children. It echoed so sadly and dismally through the gathering shadows that the marchioness nearly fell.

Père Delar supported her in his arms.

"Do you hear?" she murmured. "Do you hear?"

"Yes," Père Delar replied. "I did hear a cry."

Almost instantly the marchioness saw, or rather felt, her two boys running toward her. Their rapid, breathless steps rang out on the gravelled paths.

"Mother! mother! did you see him?" cried the elder.

"Mother! mother! did you see?" echoed the younger.

"O madame, do not listen to them," said the abbé, running behind and gasping with the effort to overtake them, their pace was so swift.

"Well, my children, what is it?" queried Madame de Chauvelin.

But the children did not reply. They simply pressed close to her side.

"Tell me what has happened," she said, caressing them. "Speak."

The boys looked at each other.

"You tell her," said the elder.

"No, you."

"Well, mamma," said the elder, "didn't you see him just the same as we did?"

"Do you hear?" cried the marchioness, raising her arms toward heaven. "Do you hear, father?"

And she grasped the Camaldule's trembling hand in her own icy cold ones.

" See whom ? " asked the monk, shuddering from head to foot.

" Why, my father," said the younger boy. "Did n't you see him, mamma ? He came from where you were, and he must have gone very near you."

" Oh ! how happy I am," said the elder boy, clapping his hands. " Papa has come back."

Madame de Chauvelin turned to the abbé.

" Madame," he said, understanding her questioning look, " I can assure you that the young gentlemen are mistaken when they say that they saw monsieur le marquis. I was close beside them, and I am sure that no one — "

" And I, monsieur," said the elder of the children, " tell you that I just saw papa as plainly as I see you."

" Fie ! Monsieur l'Abbé, for shame ! it 's wicked to tell a lie ! " said the younger boy.

" It is strange ! " said Père Delar.

The marchioness shook her head.

" They saw nothing, madame," the tutor repeated, — " nothing, absolutely nothing."

" Wait," said the marchioness.

She turned to her sons and said to them with the gentle maternal accent that makes God smile, —

" My children, you say that you saw your father ? "

" Yes, mamma," they replied with one voice.

" How was he dressed ? "

" He had his red court coat, his blue ribbon, a white waistcoat with gold embroidery, velvet breeches like his coat, silk stockings, shoes with buckles, and a sword at his side."

While the elder boy thus mentioned the details of

his father's costume, the younger nodded his head approvingly.

And while the younger boy nodded his head approvingly, Madame de Chauvelin pressed the Camaldule's hand with a more and more feverish grasp. In that same costume she had seen her husband pass.

"And was there nothing specially noticeable about your father?"

"He was very pale," said the older boy.

"Oh! yes, very pale," echoed the younger. "He looked like a dead man."

Everybody started, mother, tutor, confessor, so noticeable was the accent of terror in the child's words.

"Where was he going?" the marchioness asked at last, in a voice which she tried in vain to render firm.

"Toward the château," said the elder.

"As I was running away, I turned my head," added the other, "and I saw him going up the steps."

"Do you hear? Do you hear?" the mother whispered in the monk's ear.

"Yes, madame, I hear; but I confess that I do not understand. Why should Monsieur de Chauvelin have passed through the gate on foot, without stopping to speak to you? Why should he have passed his sons without stopping? Lastly, how can he have entered the château without any of the attendants seeing him and without asking for anybody?"

"You are right," said the abbé. "What you say is unanswerable."

"At all events," continued Père Delar, "the thing can easily be proved."

"We will go and look," cried the children, starting to run toward the château.

"And so will I." said the abbé.

" And I," murmured the marchioness.

" Madame," interposed the monk, " you are intensely agitated, white with terror, and even if it should be Monsieur de Chauvelin, — I admit that it may be he, — what occasion have you to be terrified ? "

" Father," said the marchioness, looking the monk in the face, " if he had come thus mysteriously and alone, should you not consider it a very strange proceeding ? "

" For that very reason we must all be mistaken, madame. That is why we must believe that some stranger has found his way into the grounds, a malefactor perhaps."

" But a malefactor, however much of a malefactor he may be," said the abbé, " has a body, and you would have seen that body, father, and so should I, whereas the strange part of the whole affair is that madame la marquise and these young gentlemen saw it, and that we did not see it."

" No matter," rejoined the monk. " In any event, it will be better that madame la marquise and her children retire to the orangery while we go to the château. We will call the servants and satisfy ourselves as to what has happened. Go, madame, go."

The marchioness had not strength to resist. She obeyed mechanically, and withdrew to the orangery with her sons, not having removed her eyes for an instant from the windows of the château.

" Let us pray, my sons," she said, falling on her knees, " for there is a soul entreating me to pray at this moment."

Meanwhile the monk and the abbé walked toward the château; but when they came in sight of the main door they halted, and took counsel together as to whether they should not first go to the servants' quarters and call some of the servants, who were at that time assembled for supper, to assist them in searching the buildings.

That suggestion was put forward by the prudent Camaldule, and the abbé was on the point of acceding to it when a small door was thrown open and Bonbonne, the old steward, appeared, running toward them as rapidly as his great age would permit. He was pale and trembling, gesticulating wildly, and talking to himself.

"What is it?" asked the abbé, going to meet him.

"O my God! my God!" cried Bonbonne.

"What has happened to you in heaven's name?" said the Camaldule.

"I have seen a terrible vision."

The monk and the abbé exchanged glances.

"A vision!" repeated the monk.

"Nonsense! impossible!" said the abbé.

"I tell you it is so," Bonbonne persisted.

"What was the vision? Tell us."

"Yes. What did you see?"

"I don't know yet just what I saw; but I saw — "

"Explain yourself, pray."

"Well! I was in the room where I usually work, below monsieur le marquis' large study, and connected with it, as you know, by a staircase in the wall. I was looking over the documents again to make sure that we had overlooked nothing in drawing up the will, which is so essential to the future welfare of the whole family. The clock had just struck seven. Suddenly I heard footsteps in the room overhead which I locked yesterday behind monsieur le marquis, and of which I had the key in my pocket. I listened. It was certainly footsteps. I listened again. The steps were certainly

over my head. There was some one in that room ! Nor
was that all. I heard some one open the drawers in
Monsieur de Chauvelin's desk. I heard some one move
the chair that stood in front of the desk, and that, too,
without any precaution, which seemed to me strangest
of all. My first thought was that robbers had broken
into the château. But the robbers were either very
imprudent or very sure of their game. And what was
I to do? Call the servants? They were in their
quarters at the other end of the château. While I
went to call them the robbers would have time to
escape. I took my double-barrelled gun. I went up
the secret staircase leading from my office to monsieur
le marquis' study. I walked on tiptoe. As I neared
the top steps I listened more and more intently.
Not only did I hear furniture moving, but I also heard
groaning, coughing, and various inarticulate sounds
that went to the very bottom of my soul, for I must tell
you that the nearer I came to the door the more certain
it seemed to me that I recognized monsieur le marquis'
voice."

"Strange ! " cried the abbé.

"Strange, indeed ! " the monk assented.

"Go on, Bonbonne, go on."

"At last," continued the steward, drawing nearer to
his two listeners, as if to seek a refuge with them, " at
last I looked through the keyhole and I saw a bright
light in the room, although it was quite dark outside
and the shutters were closed, closed by myself."

"Well?"

"The noise continued. There was a groaning like
the death-rattle. I hadn't a drop of blood in my veins.
However, I was determined to go on to the end. I
made an effort. I placed my eye at its post of obser-

vation once more, and I saw lighted wax candles arranged about a coffin."

"Oh! you are mad, my dear Monsieur Bonbonne," said the monk, shuddering in spite of himself.

"I saw, I saw, father."

"But your eyes deceived you," said the abbé.

"I tell you, monsieur l'abbé, that I saw the thing as plainly as I see you. I tell you that I lost neither my presence of mind nor my reason."

"And yet you fled in terror!"

"Not at all. Quite the contrary, I remained where I was, praying to God and my patron saint to give me strength. But suddenly there was a great uproar. The candles went out, and all was dark. Not till then did I come downstairs and out of doors, and see you. Now there are three of us. Here is the key to the study. You are men of the church, and consequently exempt from superstitious terror. Will you come with me? We will satisfy ourselves as to the condition of things."

"Let us go," said the Camaldule.

"Let us go," echoed the abbé.

And they entered the château together, not by the small door which had given egress to Bonbonne, but by the great door through which the marquis had entered.

As they passed through the vestibule, in front of a huge family clock surmounted by the Chauvelin arms, the steward raised the candle he had just lighted.

"Upon my word," he said, "this is very strange. Some one must have touched that clock and deranged the works."

"Why so?"

"Because it has been in the château since I was a child and has never varied."

" Well ? "

" Why, don't you see that it has stopped ? "

" At seven o'clock ! " exclaimed the monk.

" At seven o'clock ! " echoed the abbé.

And again they exchanged glances.

" Strange ! " muttered the abbé.

The monk mumbled some words which resembled a prayer.

Then they ascended the state staircase and passed through the marquis' apartments, which were closed and deserted. The vast rooms, lighted only by the flickering light of a single candle carried by the steward, were solemn and terrifying.

When they reached the door of the study their hearts were beating fast. They stopped and listened.

" Do you hear ? " asked the steward.

" Perfectly," said the abbé.

" What ? " asked the monk.

" Why, don't you hear that sort of rattle like the noise made by a person in the death agony ? "

" True," said the steward's two companions in one voice.

" I was not mistaken then ? " said the steward.

" Give me the key," said Père Delar, crossing himself. " We are men, upright men, Christians, and we should fear naught. Let us go in."

He opened the door, and, however great the man of God's trust in God, his hand trembled as he inserted the key in the lock. When the door was open, all three paused on the threshold.

The room was empty.

They walked slowly into the vast study, filled with books and pictures. Everything was in its place, except the marquis' portrait, which had broken the nail that held it and fallen from the wall, and was lying on the floor, the canvas being torn just at the head.

The abbé called the steward's attention to the portrait and breathed freely again.

"That was what caused your alarm," he said.

"Yes, that accounts for the noise," replied the steward. "But the groans we heard, — did the portrait make them ? "

"We certainly did hear groans," said the monk.

"And what is that on the table ! " cried Bonbonne, suddenly.

"What ? what is there on the table ? " asked the abbé.

"That half-extinguished candle," said Bonbonne, "that candle which is still smoking; and feel of this piece of sealing-wax, which is not yet cold."

"True ! " said the two witnesses of that almost miraculous incident.

"And this seal," continued the steward, "which monsieur le marquis wore on his watch-chain, and with which this envelope addressed to his notary, is sealed ! "

The abbé fell upon a chair more dead than alive. He had not the strength to run away.

The monk remained standing; and, without visible terror, like a man who has severed his connection with the things of this world, he tried to penetrate the mystery of whose cause he knew nothing, whose effect he saw, but whose purpose he did not understand.

Meanwhile the steward, whose devotion to his employers gave him courage, was turning over, one after another, the pages of the will he had copied the day before for his master.

When he reached the last page, the perspiration stood in beads upon his brow.

"The will is signed!" he murmured.

The abbé leaped from his chair, the monk leaned over the desk, and the steward looked from one to the other.

There was a moment of awed silence, and the bravest of the three felt his hair stand erect upon his head.

At last all three turned their eyes upon the will.

A codicil had been added, the ink being still wet.

It was conceived in these terms: —

"It is my wish that my body be interred in the Carmelite church on Place Maubert beside my ancestors.

"Done at the château of Grosbois the 27th of April, 1774, at seven o'clock in the evening.

Signed: CHAUVELIN."

The two signatures and the codicil were written in a hand less firm than that of the body of the will, but were perfectly legible.

"A *De Profundis*, messieurs," said the steward, "for it is perfectly evident that monsieur le marquis is dead."

The three men knelt piously and repeated the funeral prayer in unison. After a few moments of solemn meditation they rose.

"My poor master!" said Bonbonne. "He gave me his word to return and sign his will, and he has kept his word. God have mercy on his soul!"

The steward placed the will in the envelope, and taking up the candle, motioned to his companions to leave the room.

"There is nothing more for us to do here," he said. "Let us go and find the widow and orphans."

"You do not mean to give that package to the marchioness," said the abbé. "Oh! in heaven's name, do nothing of the kind!"

"Have no fear," said the steward. "This package shall not leave my hands except to pass into the notary's. My master has chosen me to be the executor of his will, as he has permitted me to see what I have seen, and to hear what I have heard. I shall not rest until his last wishes are executed. Then I will go and join him. Eyes that have witnessed such things should promptly close."

As he spoke, Bonbonne, having gone out last from the study, had closed and locked the door. The three went down the stairs, glanced timidly at the clock which had stopped at seven o'clock, and, passing through the door, betook themselves to the orangery where the marchioness and her children were waiting.

All three were still praying, the mother on her knees, the boys standing beside her.

"What is it?" she cried, springing hastily to her feet at sight of the three men. "What is it?"

"Continue your prayer, madame," said Père Delar. "You were not mistaken. By a special favor, granted doubtless to your piety, God vouchsafed to allow Monsieur de Chauvelin's soul to come and say farewell to us."

"O father," cried the marchioness, raising her clasped hands to heaven, "you see that my eyes did not deceive me!"

Falling once more upon her knees, she resumed her interrupted prayer, motioning to the children to follow her example.

Two hours later the sound of bells was heard in the courtyard, causing Madame de Chauvelin, who was sitting between the beds of her two sleeping children, to raise her head.

A voice rang through the corridors, shouting, —

" A courier from the king ! "

At the same moment a footman entered and handed the marchioness a long document with a black seal.

It was the official notice that the marquis had died of an attack of apoplexy at seven o'clock in the evening, while attending the king's card-party.

XII.

THE DEATH OF LOUIS XV.

AFTER Monsieur de Chauvelin's death the king was rarely seen to smile. One would have said that the marquis' ghost walked at his side wherever he went. Driving alone afforded him any distraction. Excursions were multiplied. The king went from Rambouillet to Compiègne, from Compiègne to Fontainebleau, from Fontainebleau to Versailles, but never to Paris. The king had held Paris in horror since its outbreak in connection with the baths of blood.

But all those beautiful palaces, instead of distracting his thoughts, carried him back to the past, the past to his memories, his memories to reflection. Madame du Barry alone could rouse him from that melancholy, bitter, profound reflection, and it was truly pitiful to see the pains the pretty young creature took to instil some warmth, not into the body but into the heart of the old man.

Meanwhile society was crumbling like the monarchy. To the philosophic infiltrations of Voltaire, D'Alembert, and Diderot, succeeded the scandalous cloud-bursts of Beaumarchais. Beaumarchais published his famous "Mémoire" against Councillor Goezmann, and that magistrate, a member of the Maupeou tribunal, no longer dared appear in his seat.

Beaumarchais' "Barbier de Séville" was in process of rehearsal, and people were already talking of the audacious speeches the philosopher Figaro was to deliver on the stage.

An adventure of Monsieur de Fronsac had caused much scandal. Two adventures of Monsieur le Marquis de Sade had horrified the nation.

Society could no longer be said to be walking into the abyss, but into the common sewer.

All those anecdotes were very degrading and nauseous, but they were the only ones that diverted the king. Monsieur de Sartines made him a journal of them, — another ingenious idea of Madame du Barry, — a journal which His Majesty read in the morning in his bed. That journal was edited in all the brothels of Paris, particularly at the famous La Gourdan's.

One day the king learned from his journal that Monsieur de Lorry, Bishop of Tarbes, had had the audacity on the preceding day to drive into Paris with Madame Gourdan and two of her boarders in his open carriage. That was too much. The king caused the fact to be communicated to the grand almoner, who summoned the bishop before him.

Luckily everything was explained as the merest accident, to the great glory of the prelate's modesty and chastity. On returning from Versailles the bishop of Tarbes had seen three women standing beside a broken carriage on the high road. Taking pity upon them in their embarrassment, he offered them seats in his carriage. La Gourdan thought it an amusing proposition and accepted it.

But no one was willing to believe in the prelate's innocence, and every one said to him: " What ! you don't know La Gourdan ? Really, that is incredible ! "

On top of it all the famous musical war broke out

between the Gluckists and the Piccinists. The court was divided into two factions.

The dauphiness, young, poetically inclined, naturally musical, and a pupil of Gluck, looked upon our operas as a collection of *ariettes*, more or less graceful and pleasing. After witnessing Racine's tragedies, it occurred to her to send "Iphigénie en Aulide" to her master, and to request him to pour forth the waves of his music upon Racine's harmonious lines. In six months the score was written and Gluck himself brought it to Paris.

Once in Paris Gluck became the dauphiness' favorite, and was admitted to the *petits appartements* at all hours.

One must accustom one's self to everything, and especially to the grandiose. When Gluck's music appeared, it did not create the expected impression. Empty or tired hearts do not need thought. Noise is enough for them. Thought is a bore, noise a distraction.

The old society preferred Italian music, the tinkling bell to the melodious organ.

Madame du Barry, in a spirit of opposition, and because madame la dauphine had put forward German music, became the champion of the Italian school, and sent libretti to Piccini. Piccini sent back scores, and the young and old society divided into two camps.

The fact is that entirely novel ideas were coming to light in the midst of that time-worn French society, like the strange flowers that grow between the irregular pavements of a dark courtyard or between the crumbling stones of an ancient château.

They were English ideas: Gardens with endless paths, with clumps of trees, lawns, flower-beds, and

patches of turf; life in a cottage; morning excursions
without powder or rouge, with a simple straw hat with
a broad brim and a bluebell or marguerite for ornament;
horsemen riding spirited horses, followed by jockeys
in black caps, round jackets, and leather breeches; four-
wheeled phaetons, which created a furore; princesses
dressed like shepherdesses, actresses arrayed like
queens; La Duthé, La Guimard, Sophie Arnould, La
Prairie, and La Cléophile covering themselves with diamonds, while the dauphiness, the Princesse de Lamballe,
Mesdames de Polignac, De Langeac, and D'Adhémar
aspired only to cover themselves with flowers.

And at the aspect of that new society marching on
to the unknown, Louis XV. bent his head lower and
lower. In vain did the madcap countess dance around
him, buzzing like a bee, light as a butterfly, gorgeous as
a humming-bird. From time to time he painfully raised
his heavy forehead, whereon the seal of death seemed
to be spreading more and more with every instant.

For time was flying. It was the 3d of May, and on
the 28th of June the Marquis de Chauvelin would
have been dead just two months.

And then, as if everything were conspiring to add
force to the fateful prediction, the Abbé de Beauvais
had preached at the court, and in his sermon on the
necessity of preparing for death, on the danger of
impenitence at the last, he had exclaimed, —

"Forty days more, sire, and Nineveh will be
destroyed!"

So that, after thinking of Monsieur de Chauvelin,
the king would think of the Abbé de Beauvais. So
that, after saying to the Duc d'Ayen, "On the 28th
of June Chauvelin will have been dead two months,"
he would turn to the Duc de Richelieu and mutter.

"Forty days that devilish Abbé de Beauvais said, did he not?" And he would add, "I wish that those forty days had passed."

Nor was that all. The Almanach de Liège had said, —

"In the month of April one of the most favored of women will play her last rôle."

So that Madame du Barry acted as chorus to the king's lamentations, and said of the month of April what he said of the forty days, —

"I wish that this cursed month of April had passed."

During that cursed month of April, which so alarmed Madame du Barry, and during the forty days which were the king's passion, omens multiplied. The Genoese ambassador, whom the king met frequently, died very suddenly. The Abbé de Laville, having come to his *lever* to thank him for the office of Director of Foreign Affairs which he had given him, fell at his feet stricken with apoplexy. And lastly, while the king was out hunting the lightning struck very near him.

All these occurrences made him more and more depressed.

Some hope had been entertained that the return of spring would mend matters. Nature shaking off her shroud in May, the earth taking on its robe of green, the trees donning their spring costumes, the air filled with living atoms, the fiery breaths that pass with the breezes like souls in search of bodies, — all those might well restore animation to that inert mass and power of movement to that worn-out machine.

During an outing at Trianon the king was taken ill and was, by Lamartinière's orders, removed to Versailles, where his disease was recognized as smallpox.

A malignant fever supervened and complicated the situation.

On the 29th of April the first eruption appeared, and the Archbishop of Paris, Christophe de Beaumont, hastened to Versailles.

It was a strange condition of affairs. The administration of the sacraments, if it should become necessary, could not take place *until after the expulsion of the concubine*, and that concubine, who belonged to the Jesuit party of which Christophe de Beaumont was the chief, had, as the archbishop himself had said, by bringing about the overthrow of Choiseul and the parliament, rendered such great services to the religion, that it was impossible in accordance with the canons to inflict dishonor upon her.

The leading spirits in that party were, beside Monsieur de Beaumont and Madame du Barry, the Duc d'Aiguillon, the Duc de Richelieu, the Duc de Fronsac, Maupeou, and Terray.

All of them would be overthrown by the same blow that overthrew Madame du Barry. They had no motive therefore for declaring themselves against her.

Monsieur de Choiseul's party, on the other hand, which had ramifications everywhere, even at the king's bedside, demanded the expulsion of the favorite and a speedy confession. A very curious spectacle was thus presented, for it was the party of the *philosophes*, the Jansenists, and atheists which urged the king to confess, while the Archbishop of Paris, the pious folk, and the devotees desired him to refuse to confess.

Such was the strange condition of affairs when the archbishop presented himself on the 1st of May, at half-past eleven in the morning, and asked to see the sick king.

On learning that the archbishop had arrived, poor Madame du Barry fled.

The Duc de Richelieu went to meet the prelate, whose intentions were as yet unknown to him.

"Monseigneur," said the duke, "I entreat you not to alarm the king by the *theological proposition* that has frightened so many sick people to death. But if you are curious to hear about some charming little sins, sit you down there; I will confess in the king's stead, and will tell you of some, the like of which you have not heard since you have been Archbishop of Paris. But if my suggestion does not commend itself to you, if you absolutely insist on confessing the king and repeating at Versailles the scenes in which Monsieur the Bishop of Soissons took part at Metz, if you propose to dismiss Madame du Barry with notoriety, consider the sequel and your own interests. You assure the triumph of the Duc de Choiseul, your bitterest enemy, from whom Madame du Barry was instrumental in delivering you, and you persecute your friend to the profit of your enemy, — yes, monseigneur, your friend, and so truly your friend that only yesterday she said to me, 'If the archbishop will leave us in peace he shall have his cardinal's cap; I will undertake to procure it for him and will answer for the result.' "

The Archbishop of Paris allowed Monsieur de Richelieu to say what he had to say, for although he really agreed with him, it was essential that he should seem to yield to argument. Luckily the Duc d'Aumont, Madame Adelaide, and the Bishop of Senlis joined forces with the marshal and furnished the prelate with arms against himself. He seemed to yield, promised to say nothing, entered the king's apartments, and did not mention the subject of confession; which was so satisfactory to the august patient that he immediately sent for Madame du Barry to return, and kissed her fair hands, weeping for joy.

On the next day, May 2d, the king was slightly better; Madame du Barry had sent him her two physicians, Lorry and Bordeu, instead of Lamartinière, his regular physician. They had been instructed first of all to conceal from the king the nature of his disease, to say nothing as to his condition, and especially to banish from his mind any such idea as that he was sick enough to need to have recourse to the priests.

The improvement in the king's health allowed the countess to resume for a brief space her free and easy manners, her usual mode of speech and her customary endearments. But at the very moment when, by putting forth her whole store of animal spirits, she had succeeded in making the king smile, Lamartinière, who had not been deprived of his right of access to the king's presence, appeared in the doorway, and, being highly indignant at the preference accorded Lorry and Bordeu, walked straight to the king's side, felt his pulse, and shook his head.

The king made no objection, and watched him with terror. His terror increased when he saw Lamartinière's discouraging motion.

"Well, Lamartinière?" he asked.

"Well, sire, if my brethren have not told you that you are seriously ill, they are either fools or liars."

"What do you think is the matter with me, Lamartinière?"

"*Pardieu!* sire, it is not hard to tell: Your Majesty has the smallpox."

"And you say you have no hope, my friend?"

"I do not say that, sire; a doctor never despairs. I say simply that if Your Majesty is not the Most Christian King in name only, you should look to yourself."

"Very good," said the king.

He called Madame du Barry.

"You hear, my love," he said. "I have the small-pox, and it is a very dangerous disease, firstly, because of my age, and secondly, because of my other troubles. Lamartinière has just reminded me that I am the Most Christian King and the oldest son of the Church, my love. Perhaps we shall have to separate. I wish to prevent a scene like the one at Metz. Tell the Duc d'Aiguillon what I say to you, so that you and he can arrange for our parting quietly if I grow worse."

When the king was speaking thus, the whole Choiseul faction was beginning to complain aloud, accusing the archbishop of complaisance, and saying that he would allow the king to die without the sacraments in order not to disturb Madame du Barry.

These charges reached Monsieur de Beaumont's ears, and he, in order to put an end to them, determined to take up his residence at Versailles, in the convent of the Lazarists, to make an impression on the public, and be in a position to take advantage of the most favorable moment for his religious ceremonies, in order not to sacrifice Madame du Barry until the king's condition should be altogether desperate.

It was on the 3d of May that the archbishop returned to Versailles. Having arrived there, he waited.

Meanwhile, scandalous scenes were being enacted at the king's bedside. The Cardinal de la Roche-Aymon was of the same mind as the Archbishop of Paris, and desired that everything should be done quietly; but it was not so with the Bishop of Carcassonne, who played the zealot, renewing the scene at Metz years before, and crying from the housetops *that the sacraments must be administered to the king, that the concubine must be driven forth, that the canons of the church must be enforced, and that the king must set an example to Europe and Christian France, which he had scandalized.*

"What right have you to force your opinions on me?" cried Monsieur de la Roche-Aymon, testily.

The bishop took the pastoral cross from his neck and put it almost under the prelate's nose.

"The right that this cross gives me," he said. "Learn to respect that right, monseigneur, and do not allow your king to die without the sacraments of the church, whose eldest son he is."

All this took place in Monsieur d'Aiguillon's presence. He realized what scandal such a discussion would cause if it should become public.

He entered the king's apartment.

"Well, duke, have you carried out my orders?"

"With regard to Madame du Barry, sire?"

"Yes."

"I preferred to wait until Your Majesty should repeat them. I shall never be in haste to separate the king from those who love him."

"Thanks, duke, but it must be done. Take the poor countess and escort her quietly to your country estate at Rueil. I shall be grateful to Madame d'Aiguillon for any attention she may show her."

Despite that very explicit command, Monsieur d'Aiguillon was still loath to hasten the favorite's departure, and concealed her in the château, announcing that she was to go on the following day. That announcement moderated the ecclesiastical exigencies to some extent.

It was a happy idea on the Duc d'Aiguillon's part, as it turned out, to keep Madame du Barry at Versailles, for, during the day of the fourth of May, the king asked for her so persistently that the duke confessed that she was still there.

"Send for her, then, send for her," cried the king.

And so Madame du Barry returned to the bedside for the last time.

The countess left Versailles weeping bitterly. The poor creature, who was good-hearted, amiable, and easy-going, loved Louis XV. as one loves a father.

Madame d'Aiguillon took Madame du Barry and her sister Mademoiselle du Barry in her carriage, and drove them to Rueil to await the result.

She was hardly out of the courtyard, when the king asked for her again.

"She has gone," he was told.

"Gone?" echoed the king; "then it is time for me to go too. Order prayers to be said at Sainte-Géneviève."

Monsieur de la Vrillière at once wrote to the parliament, which body had the right, in extreme cases, to order the ancient relic to be opened or closed.

The 5th and 6th of May passed without any mention of confession, viaticum, or extreme unction. The curé of Versailles presented himself with the purpose of preparing the king for that pious ceremony; but he fell in with the Duc de Fronsac, who gave him his *word as a gentleman* that he would throw him out of the window at the first word he uttered on the subject.

"If I am not killed by the fall, I shall come in again at the door," said the curé, "for it is my right."

But on the 7th, at three o'clock in the morning, the king himself imperatively demanded the presence of Abbé Mandoux, a poor priest with no taste for intrigue, a worthy ecclesiastic who had been given him for a confessor, and who was blind.

His confession lasted seventeen minutes.

The confession at an end, the Ducs de la Vrillière and D'Aiguillon attempted to delay the viaticum, but Lamar-

tinière, who had a special enmity against Madame du
Barry because she had induced the king to take up with
Lorry and Bordeu, approached the king and said : —

"I have seen Your Majesty in very difficult positions,
sire, but I have never admired you as I do to-day. If you
follow my advice you will finish at once what you have
begun so well."

Thereupon the king ordered Mandoux to be recalled,
and Mandoux gave him absolution.

As for the notorious atonement that was to crush
Madame du Barry in solemn form, it was not mentioned.
The grand almoner and the archbishop had agreed upon
this formula which was proclaimed in presence of the
sacred host : —

*Although the king need account for his conduct to
God alone, he declares that he repents having caused
scandal among his subjects, and that he desires to live
henceforth only to maintain the religion and the happiness of his people.*

The royal family, increased by Madame Louise, who
had come forth from her convent to care for her father,
received the sacrament at the foot of the staircase.

While the king was receiving the sacraments, the
dauphin, who was kept at a distance because he had not
had the smallpox, wrote as follows to Abbé Terray : —

"MONSIEUR LE CONTRÔLEUR-GÉNÉRAL, — I beg you to
cause two hundred thousand francs to be distributed among
the poor in the various parishes of Paris, to pray for the
king. If you deem this too much, deduct it from the allow-
ances of madame la dauphine and myself.

Signed :   LOUIS-AUGUSTE."

During the 7th and 8th the patient grew worse. The
king felt that his body was literally being torn in strips.

Abandoned by his courtiers, who dared not remain beside that living corpse, he had no other attendants than his three daughters, who did not leave him for an instant.

The king was terrified. In the horrible gangrene that attacked his whole body he saw a direct chastisement of heaven. To his mind the invisible hand that marked him with black spots was God's hand. In an access of delirium, all the more terrible because it was not the delirium of fever but of the thought, he saw flames, he saw the burning pit, and he called to his confessor, the poor blind priest, his only refuge, to hold the crucifix between him and the fiery lake. Then he would himself take the holy water, he himself would raise sheets and coverlids, he himself, with groans of terror, would pour the holy water over his whole body, then he would demand the crucifix, take it in both hands, kiss it fervently, and cry: "O Lord! Lord! intercede for me, the greatest sinner that ever lived."

In such terrible despairing agony he passed the whole day of the 9th. During that day, which was naught but one long confession, neither the priest nor his daughters left him. His body was eaten by the most disgusting gangrene, and the corpse-like king, still living, exhaled such an odor that two servants fell to the floor asphyxiated, and one of them died.

On the 10th, in the morning, his thigh-bones could be seen through the cracks in the flesh; three other servants fainted. Terror invaded Versailles. The whole household fled. There were no living beings in the palace save the three noble-hearted girls and the excellent priest.

The whole day of the 10th was one long agony. The king, already dead, could not make up his mind to die; you would have said that he was trying to throw himself out of bed, anticipating the fall. At last, at five minutes to three, he drew himself up, held out his hands, fixed his eyes upon a certain point of the wall and cried: —

"Chauvelin! Chauvelin! it is not two months yet — " Then he fell back and died.

Great as was the courage with which God had filled the hearts of the three princesses and the priest, when the king was dead they deemed their task at an end; furthermore, all three of the princesses were infected with the disease that had killed the king.

The arrangements for the obsequies were intrusted to the grand master, who arranged everything without entering the palace.

No one could be found save the night-cart men of Versailles who dared place the king in the leaden coffin which was prepared for him. He was laid in that last abode, without ointment or essences, rolled in the sheets of the bed in which he died; then the leaden coffin was placed in a wooden casket and carried into the chapel.

On the 12th of May, what had been Louis XV. was taken to Saint-Denis; the coffin was in a large hunting carriage. A second carriage was occupied by the Duc d'Ayen and the Duc d'Aumont; in the third were the grand almoner and the curé of Versailles. The funeral procession consisted of a score of pages and about fifty grooms on horseback.

The cortége started from Versailles at eight in the evening and arrived at Saint-Denis at eleven. The body was lowered into the royal vault whence it was not to come forth until the day of the profanation of Saint-Denis, and the entrance to the vault was not only closed but caulked, so that no emanation from that human

10

carrion should make its way from the abode of the dead into the abodes of the living.

We have described elsewhere the glee of the Parisian populace at the death of Louis XIV. Their glee was no less great when they found that they were rid of him whom they had, thirty years earlier, named the Well-Beloved.

Some one rallied the curé of Sainte-Géneviève concerning the efficacy of the relic.

" What do you complain of ? " he retorted. " Is he not dead ? "

On the next day, Madame du Barry at Rueil received a letter of banishment.

Sophie Arnould learned at the same time of the king's death and the banishment of the favorite.

" Alas ! " said she, " we have no father or mother now."

That was the only funeral discourse pronounced over the tomb of the grandson of Louis XIV.